Dedication

To Jeff and Mary Telker

Acknowlegement

I was struggling to find a plot for the next Whistling Pines book when Julie, my wife, suggested a mystery built around a city festival. She found a website for the Two Harbors (California) Buccaneer Days celebration. I fired off an email to my trusted experts, Brian Johnson and Deanna Wilson who brainstormed ideas. They helped form random thoughts into a cohesive plot and kept me from writing myself into a corner. In addition to their crazy ideas, I solicited variants on the pirate theme from consultants Frannie Brozo and Mike Westfall. Within a week the four of them had me swimming in shady characters and plot twists. Without their ideas, suggestions, and support, I'd still be staring at a blank page.

Thanks to Anne Flagge, Jeff Telker, and Natalie Lund for proofreading.

Thanks also to Jude Pittman and the people at BWL Publishing for their guidance and support.

"The coldest winter I ever spent was a summer in Duluth."
-Mark Twain

Chapter One

In my role as recreation director of Whistling Pines Senior Residence, I'm responsible for providing activities to engage and entertain the residents. We have a number of repetitive things like Monday bingo, Tuesday singalong, Wednesday pie day, and Thursday movies, but there's always keen interest in something new. I was in my office pondering the options for the Thursday movie when I felt a presence at my door.

Before I could turn to see who was there, Brian Johnson, the tuba player from the Two Harbors band, swept into the room and sat in my chair. "How much does pirate sweetcorn cost?"

I shrugged.

"Buck an ear." When I didn't burst out laughing, he explained. "Get it? Pirates are buccaneers."

I smiled politely, giving him the same reaction I get from my very proper mother-in-law when I tell her a joke.

"Doc, have you heard about the chamber of commerce plan to bring in more tourists?"

I shook my head. "I've been a little distracted. Jenny's about ten months pregnant and she's not sleeping much, which means I'm not sleeping much."

Brian's cherubic smile spread across his face. "Think of it as practice for dealing with a newborn baby."

"Howard Johnson told me it'll get worse."

Brian nodded. "That was my experience." He pointed to my computer monitor. "Let's get back to the tourists. Pull up the Two Harbors city webpage."

I typed in a search screen and clicked on the city's homepage. "What now?"

"The icon in the bottom right corner is the chamber of commerce link. Click it."

My computer screen suddenly filled with a pirate ship background and message about Buccaneer Days overlaying a ship logo. The page was dotted with links to lodging, restaurants, activities, and the date. I looked twice because it said the festival was only a few days away. "That's a misprint. It's next year, right?"

Brian shook his head. "They just announced that it's this coming Saturday."

"Nobody sets up a festival and gets tourists to attend in less than a week."

Brian's grin told me there was something I'd missed. "Go back to your search screen and type in 'Two Harbors Buccaneer Days.'"

I typed in the search and clicked on the link. The screen was different from the chamber of commerce page, but also featured a pirate ship and same date but included scantily clad wenches posing on the ship's deck. "Why are there two websites?"

"This one is for Two Harbors on Catalina Island."

I checked the page finding nothing to indicate the location until I saw the contact phone number with a California prefix instead of the northern Minnesota 218 area code. I stared at the Catalina Island list of activities and contests, envious of their organizing team's vision. "I'm missing something."

"Well, since the Covid-19 thing is over, people are starting to come out of their houses and are looking for things to do. They're apparently searching the names of Minnesota's North Shore communities, looking for summer activities. When they type in *Two Harbors Summer Festivals,* they hit the California Two Harbors website. It looks interesting and fun, so they're booking hotels, inns, B&Bs. A few motels called our chamber of commerce, requesting information. After a half dozen phone calls, Meg Cochran at the chamber of commerce did her own search and hit the California website. She called an emergency meeting of the membership and they decided to capitalize on the misdirected festival interest. Since hotels from Duluth to Silver Bay were already booked with Buccaneer Days reservations, they decided to create a city festival."

I groaned. "The town is going to be a zoo."

"The Two Harbors city band is moving the August Sousa Concert to this weekend. We're going to pass the hat to help pay off the debt on the new bandshell." He paused and looked at me hopefully. "We need a piccolo player for Stars and Stripes Forever."

"No. I did it once and that's it."

"Doc, the little girl who did the duet with you moved. We need you."

There was another disturbance at my door and Jenny's voice chimed in. "Who needs Peter?"

"The band needs him. We're doing a Sousa concert during the pirate festival."

"You can do that, Peter. I'm fine. Just bring your cellphone in case I go into labor."

"No, I don't want to play piccolo." I paused and turned to Jenny. "Did you know about Two Harbor's Buccaneer Days?"

"There's a full-page ad in this morning's newspaper. They're having costume contests, a talk like a pirate contest, and the newspaper is awarding a prize for the best pirate joke."

I groaned and looked at Brian. "The cost of pirate corn is *not* a winner."

Jenny stepped into my tiny office. There was barely enough room between her baby-swollen abdomen for three of us.

Brian looked at Jenny. "What's pirate corn cost?"

Jenny shrugged. "I don't know."

I held my head in my hands while Brian answered, "Buck an ear."

Jenny giggled. "That's clever. It could be a winner."

I looked up. "Don't encourage him."

"Peter, see if they make pirate wench maternity costumes?" Jenny asked, pointing to my computer screen.

"Are you kidding? You can't stand for ten minutes and you have to pee every thirty minutes."

Jenny's expression told me I'd crossed a line. I typed in the search and got three hits. "It looks like there's a site that guarantees two-day delivery."

"Order one, then pick a costume for yourself."

"Really?"

I felt a nudge. Brian was grinning silently. He was never quiet, but he knew the exchange between Jenny and me was too precious to interrupt.

"I'm on it. Do you want the one that looks like a pregnant pirate t-shirt or one with that shows a lot of cleavage?"

"I plan on wearing it to work…"

"Aah, the pregnant pirate t-shirt."

Jenny left and Brian leaned close to me. "You slipped up a couple times there. You'll know the correct answers after you've been married for a few years." Brian stood, patted my shoulder, then stopped at the door. "Find the piccolo. I think Jenny expects you to play." Then he disappeared.

I stared at the California website for a few minutes before inspiration stuck me. I switched to my word processing software and started typing. Within ten minutes, I'd written announcements for talk like a pirate, best pirate costume, best pirate's wench costume, and a find the pirate's booty contests for Whistling Pines.

Nancy, the director, was sitting in her office when I knocked on the door. "Do you have a second?"

Nancy waved me in, smiling. "Sure, what's up?"

I handed her the announcements and sat in her guest chair. "I don't know if you've heard about the pirate festival in town…"

Nancy flipped through the pages I'd printed, grinning. "The chamber of commerce called and asked if we could contribute toward advertising and prizes. I couldn't see how we'd get involved, but this sounds like fun for the residents. Well done."

I was collecting the sheets when her phone rang. She looked at the caller ID and put up a finger, signaling for me to wait. I heard half of a conversation that involved a lot of head nodding and the repeated phrase, "I'm sure he'd be happy to." Being the only male member of the staff, other than the elderly maintenance man, I had a sinking feeling I was being volunteered for something.

Nancy ended the call and smiled at me. "That was the mayor. The band director asked him to twist your arm. They need a piccolo player for the band concert Saturday night. I told him you'd be happy to play."

"But…"

Nancy put up her hand and leaned on her desk. "We are part of this community and there aren't many opportunities for us to contribute in a visible role. The band director promised to introduce you as the representative from Whistling Pines."

I raised my eyebrows. "I'm not sure where the piccolo is. We moved into Dolores' house, and I haven't seen it since I packed up to move."

"You'd better find it and start practicing."

Wendy, the vivacious, energetic assistant director swept into Nancy's office without knocking. She's musically versatile, able to sing anything from Gospel to jazz, and has a heavenly alto voice. She also loved to make me squirm. "I heard we're having a pirate's wench costume contest."

I nodded and handed her the announcement. "It's intended for the residents, not the staff."

11

Wendy's eyes sparkled mischievously. "I can't compete for a prize, but I can still wear my costume."

"You have a pirate wench costume?" I asked.

"I bought one for a Halloween party a couple tears ago. I found an...adult costume." She spun and disappeared.

I looked at Nancy, hoping I'd misinterpreted Wendy's comment. "Do you think she means one in an adult size, or that she has an *adult* costume?"

Nancy looked at me like a dense child. "It's Wendy. I'd guess her costume fits in both categories."

Closing my eyes, I said, "I was going to take pictures for our advertising."

"You might want to learn how to photoshop Wendy out of the pictures." Nancy stood, signaling the end of our conversation. "Just in case."

"You know, this festival is going to bring a whole new level of craziness to town."

Wendy, overhearing me, popped her head around the corner. Her grin was devilish. "Hmm, a bunch of drunk pirates. What's the worst that could happen?"

As it turned out, she was prophetic. The worst happened.

Chapter Two

The aroma of pipe smoke preceded Len Rentz into my office. The trim, gray-haired police chief was a long-time friend. Although I'd never admit it to him, I enjoyed his occasional requests to assist with investigations. No, I didn't want to be a cop. But yes, it was mentally challenging and interesting to poke around the edges of an investigation and to feel like I'd contributed to solving the crime.

"What's up, Len?"

Len cupped his smoldering pipe in his left hand. I no longer admonished him about the laws against smoking inside, having realized he was the person I'd have to report the infraction to. He leaned back with a sparkle in his eyes I hadn't seen in years. "I've decided to retire."

"Are you serious?"

"I am. There's no point in my hanging around any longer. The job is just not worth the bother anymore, and I've decided to take my pension and kick back."

"I think it's a tougher transition than you expect. You'll be going from a busy responsible position to perpetual vacation."

Len nodded. "I'm looking forward to that. I think I'll go fishing this summer, then maybe we'll check out Arizona and Florida this winter."

I put out my hand and we shook. "Congratulations. How's the city council going to replace you?"

"I told them there's no one on the force better than your friend, Kerry Stone. I expect they'll vote on offering him the chief's job tonight."

"Does he want the job?"

Len grinned. "His Army investigative experience made him a hell of a cop. He's spinning his wheels writing speeding tickets and arresting drunken snowmobilers. He was an Army major and is well prepared for the chief's position, probably better prepared than I was for dealing with the politics of the job. On top of that, he understands the computer technology and speaks the language of the medical examiner and the forensics people."

"I assume you decided to pull the plug now, during the summer, so you can unwind by doing things outdoors."

Len got a cagey smile. "I heard about Buccaneer Days and decided to get out before that craziness."

"Really, that's what pushed you over the edge?"

Len stood and nodded. "I don't need to live through the nightmare of coordinating agencies, planning emergency responses, patrolling crowds, dealing with drunken pirates, and the debauchery that comes with the alcohol and crowds."

A vision of a thousand pirate-costume-clad people milling around town flashed through my brain. I briefly considered taking Jenny and Jeremy on a vacation. I realized Len was still standing in the door, and I snapped back to reality. "I'll call Kerry tomorrow and offer my congratulations."

I could tell Len had something else on his mind, so I waited. "I'm asking a few people to come by Judy's tomorrow afternoon for a cup of coffee and slice of pie. Would you and Jenny..."

"We'll be there. Is there anything else I can do for you?"

Len's eyes teared up and he put out his hand. Instead of shaking my hand, he pulled me out of my seat and wrapped his arms around me and we hugged. "If I'd had a son, I'd hoped he'd be like you."

I was speechless as he released the hug, spun around, and walked away. I was still staring at the door when Jenny's head popped in. She was surprised to see me in tears. "Are you okay?"

I still didn't trust my voice, so just nodded.

She pushed past me and sat in my guest chair. "What's with the tears?"

I sat down and took a deep breath. "Len's retiring and he's recommended Kerry Stone be appointed police chief."

"Kerry, the veteran with the terrible burns who has a kid Jeremy's age?"

"Yeah. Len thinks he's up to the job."

"I'll have to look up their number and invite them over for supper." When I didn't offer my immediate support, Jenny reached out and took my hand. "What else?"

"Len's hosting a retirement party for a few people at Judy's tomorrow afternoon. We're invited."

"Okay, but that's not what brought those tears."

"Len hugged me and told me he wished he'd had a son like me."

Jenny, whose pregnant body was a teapot of raging hormones always on the brink of boiling over, burst into tears. I handed her a box of tissues and let her sob until she blew her nose and handed the box back. "That's...so special. What are you getting him for a retirement gift?"

I drew a blank, which apparently showed on my face.

Jenny got up. "I'll pick up something on my way home."

"Like what?"

Jenny tipped her head back in thought. "I'm not sure, but I'll come up with something." With that, she was gone.

Wendy was at my door before I sat. "I heard Len Rentz is retiring and Kerry Stone is replacing him."

16

Jenny hadn't been gone long enough to tell anyone, so I knew Wendy had another source. "Who told you that?"

Wendy's eyes sparkled. "I think you just confirmed the rumor."

"Crap."

Wendy, grinning from ear-to-ear, walked away.

* * *

Jeremy was sitting at the dining room table with a half-full glass of milk, a plate covered with crumbs, a dirty backpack, and a pile of worksheets. He barely looked up when I walked in.

"How's the homework?" I asked.

"It's fine." He shoved his worksheet away. "I don't know why we're still in school, Dad. It's summer."

"The school district extended the school year to make up for the snow days you got off this winter."

"It's not fair. School should be done." Jeremy got up and leaned on the doorframe as I dug through the refrigerator, taking out makings for a green salad and meatballs for spaghetti. "Do you *have to* make a salad?"

"We need the vitamins and minerals in vegetables."

"We didn't eat salads at your house before you married Mom."

17

Busted, I smiled. "Now I'm smarter about eating."

"I liked it better when you didn't know about salads. I like the pizzas and hamburgers you used to make all the time."

With the meatballs in a frying pan and water heating for pasta, I took a break and knelt down eye to eye with Jeremy. "I like those things too, but your mom is smarter than me and she knew we needed more vegetables in our diet than I was cooking."

Jeremy was unconvinced. "Mom says you're the smartest person she's ever met, smarter than her."

"I don't think anyone's smarter than your mom." I saw an opportunity and grabbed it. "There's going to be another person in our house shortly. How are we going to welcome the baby?"

The baby was a tense subject Jeremy avoided. His answer was a shrug.

"Do you think it's a boy or a girl?"

"Mom said you didn't want to know until the baby arrived."

"We don't know. Would you rather have a brother or sister?"

He shrugged.

"Baseballs and bats, or Barbie dolls?"

"Eww. Barbie dolls, Really?"

"If the baby is a girl, she'll like dolls."

"Do we have to keep it? I mean, there's already three of us. I like that."

"It's too late to change the arrival. We'll all have to adapt."

Jeremy wrinkled his nose. "If we have to keep it, I hope it's a boy. At least he could play catch with me."

I felt pleased the door to discussion had opened. "We need to welcome the baby regardless of its sex."

Jeremy shrugged. "I heard lots of people want to adopt babies."

I laughed. "We're not putting your sibling up for adoption. We'll love the baby just like we love you."

"Jacob says you'll spend all your time with the baby. I'm not your real kid and the baby will be."

Jacob Stone, the son of a Iraq vet, and Jeremy became close friends after the Christmas ghost incidents. Jacob was Jeremy's information source for family dynamics, siblings, and possibly sex education.

The grenade was on the ground and I had to jump on it. "Babies are a lot of work, but I'll never love you any less. You're my son and that won't change because a baby arrives." I reached out and pulled Jeremy into a hug before he could squirm away. He was as rigid as a board, then I felt his hands on my back, followed by him relaxing in my grip.

"Dad?"

"Yeah."

"Do I have to share my room with the baby?"

"The baby will have its own room. Your room is your room."

"Rusty O'Brien has to share a room with his brother."

"Even if the baby is a boy, he'll have a room and you'll have a room."

Jeremy let out a breath and drew in another. "Mom said you made the baby with her."

"Yes," I said, assuming Jacob planted ideas that were making connections in Jeremy's mind. I braced for the obvious follow-up question and tried to frame an answer about the anatomy of baby creation in terms he'd understand.

"Why?"

I relaxed. "Because people in love often have babies."

"Who made me with Mom? Did he love her?"

This topic wasn't a grenade. It was a bomb. Jenny got pregnant just after she graduated from high school. Jeremy's father had been a pilot, training with the Air Force in Duluth, and had returned home before he knew she was pregnant. "I never knew him. I think he loved her, but he let me be your dad. Your real dad."

"But..." the rest of the question died.

"No buts. I'm your real dad, your only dad. It says so on your birth certificate." I held him back and looked into his eyes. "Okay?"

The kitchen door opened behind us. "What's okay?" Jenny asked.

I knew Jeremy wouldn't talk about what we'd just discussed. "Just guy talk." I let go of Jeremy and pushed him toward the table. "Now, homework."

Jenny set down a bag and walked to me, hugging over her pregnant belly. "Baby discussions?" she asked in a whisper.

I nodded.

"He's having trouble with this."

I glanced at Jeremy. "I think we've knocked down a couple hurdles."

"Like what?"

"We're not going to put the baby up for adoption, and Jeremy keeps his own room."

Jenny leaned back and looked into my eyes. "He thought we'd put the baby up for adoption?"

"I think it was just something he'd heard at school. It's okay."

Jenny's eyes teared up and she buried her face in my shoulder. "I'm as big as a house, I pee in my pants a little every time I sneeze, I'm struggling to work, and…Jeremy thinks we should put the baby up for adoption."

Jeremy reacted to the whispering of his name and perked up and came over to us. "What's wrong?"

Jenny tousled his hair. "The baby won't replace you. He or she will just be an addition to the love we all share. Will that be okay?"

Jeremy shrugged. "I guess. Do I really have to eat a salad, or can I just have spaghetti and meatballs?"

Jenny laughed at the sudden change of focus. "Eat one bite of salad, that's all I demand."

Jeremy drew a deep breath and blew it out. "If I have to." Then he went back to his homework.

The sizzle of meatballs in the frying pan caught my attention and I scrambled to find a spatula to roll them over. Jenny was at my side. "I think he's okay with this."

"It's an adjustment for all of us. Go change out of your scrubs and I'll have supper on the table by the time you come downstairs."

Chapter Three

The morning dew was thick on my windshield and I let the windshield wipers clear it while I waited for the heater to produce warm air. We were approaching the summer solstice, leading to the warmest time of the year, yet the overnight Two Harbors temperature was forty-eight degrees (9° C). We lived next to Lake Superior, a body of deep cold water the weather forecasters called the giant air conditioner. The depths of the lake were always just a degree above freezing, and the surface barely warmed ten or twenty degrees above that, even in the hottest days of August.

The morning rush hour consisted of three cars in line for coffee at the McDonalds drive-through. I met a semi loaded with pulpwood destined for the Cloquet paper mill and a contractor's pickup pulling a white trailer sporting the logo *Sam Fixes Anything*.

Whistling Pines was quiet. The overnight receptionist looked up from her Sudoku and nodded as I passed. I was hanging my fleece on a hook behind my office door when the phone rang. The caller I.D. said *THCofC*. That told me nothing aside from the fact that the call originated in Two Harbors. I glanced at my empty coffee cup, considering a trip to

23

the dining room for coffee instead of answering a call from an unknown caller. My curiosity got the best of me. I identified myself and prepared for a sales pitch I could quickly disconnect.

"Peter Rogers?" The female voice sounded familiar, but I couldn't identify the caller.

"Yes, who is this?"

"Meg Cochran, from the chamber of commerce. Nancy, your director, suggested I give you a call."

My hopes for coffee sank as I sat in my chair. "What did Nancy have in mind?"

"The chamber is struggling to put together the Buccaneer Days festival for the weekend. We're asking each chamber of commerce member to provide someone to help with the planning."

"Crap."

Meg burst into laughter before I realized I'd uttered the oath out loud. "Your candid response is a refreshing bit of honesty after a dozen calls to people who've agreed to help but will probably contribute little or nothing to the effort."

"I'm sorry that slipped out."

"Don't apologize. Hell, I've heard and said worse than that."

I remembered a chamber meeting when I'd filled in for Nancy. Meg solicited volunteers for the winter gala, a fundraiser sponsored by the chamber to raise money for scholarships given to the top Two Harbors high school seniors. When no one offered to assist, Meg went on a tirade that reminded me of a Marine Corps sergeant urging on his reluctant squad.

"What did Nancy offer?"

"Actually, I need you to provide the part that's been the most difficult for me. Nancy said you were extremely creative and came up with a constant stream of interesting activities for Whistling Pines. I've got a dozen people who will help us arrange and coordinate activities, but aside from looking at the Catalina Island Buccaneer Days website, we don't have a clue what activities make sense for a Two Harbors festival. Will you help me?"

I opened the computer and started a search for Buccaneer Days. "Can you give me a couple days to think about this. I'll be happy to help, but I need some time to write down a few ideas."

"Peter, time is my most precious commodity. We're less than a week away from the advertised dates and I need your ideas right now." Meg paused. "How about this? Give me the first two things that come to mind, and I'll get my volunteers started on them. Call me this afternoon with whatever else you've got, and we'll roll with it."

"Um..."

"Two ideas, Peter. Please."

"We're going to have a costume contest here at Whistling Pines. I suppose a best pirate and best pirate's wench costume contest would be at the top of my list."

"Great! Give me another."

"The city band is moving their Sousa concert to Saturday night."

I heard the clicking of Meg's fingers on a keyboard. "We've already got that in our plans. Try again."

"Meg, I need to think."

"One more, please."

I drew a deep breath as the Catalina Two Harbors website came up on my computer screen. Pictures of a pirate ship, loaded with scantily-clad wenches wielding cutlasses popped up, with a list of bands who'd be playing concerts through the four-day festival.

"Okay, I've a couple things. Do you know anyone who has a sailboat they can rig to look like a pirate ship?"

"Not offhand, but I'll call the yacht club. What else?"

The phrase "yacht club" spurred a thought. "Suggest the yacht club put on a sailboat race, a regatta."

"Great! Anything else?"

"We did a scavenger hunt and that was a fiasco, so I don't recommend that. How about a pirate's treasure hunt. Hide a gold coin, from the pirate's treasure chest, and offer a $100 prize to whomever finds it. Put clues in the newspaper or give them out on the radio station."

"Got it! I'll talk to the city and we'll limit it to public property so the treasure hunters aren't ripping up people's yards. It'll be like the St. Paul Winter Carnival medallion hunt."

I let out a sigh of relief. "Is that enough?"

"It's enough to get us started, but please don't quit. Call me back this afternoon with any more ideas that pop to mind."

I was clicking through the icons on the Catalina Island website and stalled on one. "I can't believe this. The Catalina Buccaneers Day does a naturist sunbathing cruise." I chuckled. "That's something we can take off the list. There's no way anyone would sign up for a June naked sunbathing cruise on Lake Superior. The fishermen are still wearing snowmobile suits." Meg didn't laugh that idea off and I thought she'd hung up.

"I've got a friend who's a nudist. He's mentioned taking sailboat charters out of Duluth. I'll ask how many people they can take at a time."

"Meg, I was kidding."

"I'll call and see if he's willing to arrange something."

"No, Meg. Really, I was kidding. It's a very bad idea." I was listening to a dial tone.

I hung up the phone and grabbed my coffee mug, stewing over the assignment to assist the chamber of commerce. I'd cooled off by the time I reached the dining room and concluded I'd dodged a bullet by being asked to generate ideas, not to execute them.

A half-dozen early diners were sipping coffee and eating cereal and fruit. I waved at them and drew a cup of coffee from the urn. Wendy was sitting at a table in a far corner with the tablecloth turned back. She was hunched over a crossword puzzle, deep in thought. I tried to slip out of the dining room unnoticed, but she waggled her finger, beckoning me to join her.

"What's up?" I asked, taking the chair across from her

"I need a ten-letter word for bumbling incompetent. The third letter is an N."

"Nincompoop," I replied.

Wendy paused, trying to discern if I seriously knew the answer, or if I was just making up a word to irritate her. I didn't break into a grin, so she penciled in the word. "Why do you remember words like that?"

"You've heard people called nincompoops."

"Not since my grandparents died. It's not something that comes up in everyday conversations. "*Say, Ida, have you seen that nincompoop today?*"

I stood up. "That's all you needed?"

She glanced around, then waved me back into the chair. Leaning close, she asked, "What's the deal with the naked cruise?"

"I have no idea what you're talking about."

"Cut the crap, Peter. There's a sign-up sheet on the bulletin board."

I felt the blood drain from my face. "There's no boat. There's no cruise."

"It doesn't matter. You know if something is circulating in the rumor mill, it's assumed to be true until proven otherwise."

"Who started the rumor?"

A sly grin crept across Wendy's face. "I overheard Helen Rosencrantz tell Hulda Packer there was a naturist cruise on the Two Harbors Buccaneers Days website. Hulda got all excited about a birdwatching cruise until Helen explained a naturist is a person who likes to vacation without clothing."

"Okay. How did that become a sign-up sheet?"

"Bud overheard them and rushed off. Next thing I knew, there was a handwritten sign-up sheet for a naked cruise on the bulletin board."

"Has anyone but Bud signed up?"

The evil smile was back. "Last time I checked, the list was full."

I closed my eyes and let out a sigh. "Who else signed up?"

"Besides me?"

"What? You signed up for a clothing optional cruise?"

"I thought I could use a little color. It's been a long winter and my tan has faded."

"Let me guess, you want to tan and not get tan lines."

Wendy smiled. "People keep asking about my tattoos and I can't really show them here. Well, not without getting fired."

"I'm taking down the sign-up list."

Wendy shrugged. "There'll be a new one tomorrow."

"It makes no difference, there is no naturist cruise."

"There will be some very disappointed people."

I stalked out of the dining room, only to be confronted by Hulda Packer, who ran her walker into my path. "Peter, I'm not interested in going on a cruise naked, but if you could set up a second cruise for birdwatching, I'd sign up for that in a minute."

Brian Johnson slipped behind Hulda, grinning like a Cheshire cat. "Yeah, maybe the boats could sail side-by-side. I'll buy binoculars if you arrange that."

I grabbed Brian's arm and steered him away from Hulda. "I'd appreciate it if you'd stop throwing gas on the flames." Then I hesitated. "You didn't tell a tuba joke."

"I'm transitioning to pirate jokes."

I groaned. "Like buck an ear pirate corn."

He nodded. "There's going to be a pirate joke competition, so I'm not going to waste my good material around here. You might steal it."

"Trust me, I won't steal your jokes."

Considering that for a moment, Brian leaned close. "What did the pirate say when his wooden leg got stuck in the freezer? Shiver me timbers."

"You're right. You're not wasting any good jokes on me."

Brian was on my heels as I walked back to my office. "I do have something important to tell you."

"What?"

"The city council vote for the new police chief wasn't unanimous for Kerry Stone."

I stopped in front of the bulletin board. *Naked Cruise Sign Up* was scrawled in big red letters, followed by lines filled with signatures. I pulled down the sign. "He won the vote."

"Yes, but the one dissenter wasn't happy."

"Why?"

"Phyllis Comstock wants a kinder and friendlier police force, and she thinks Kerry looks too militant."

"Who did she propose?"

Brian became uncharacteristically quiet. "Um, me."

"She wanted you to be the police chief? Do you have a criminology degree?"

"No, but she thought having a pudgy, smiling police chief would project a kinder image for Two Harbors."

"I hope you jumped up and told them you weren't interested."

Brian looked away. "I told them I'd consider it if I could hire three more cops who were a trumpet player, a drummer, and an accordionist."

"You told them you'd be the police chief if they let you hire a band?"

"It'd be the Two Harbors Police Band."

"Did you get laughed out of the council chambers?"

Brian bit his lip. "Actually, Gunnar Svedberg changed his vote from Kerry to me."

I threw up my hands. "That's the stupidest thing I've ever heard!"

Brian's sudden smile made me uneasy. "Got you, Doc." He turned and left.

"That was all a big joke? Well, it wasn't funny!"

Jenny dashed out of Nancy's office. Well, she moved quickly—pregnant women don't really dash. "What's not funny?"

Deciding not to repeat Brian's stupid attempt to provoke me, I held up the naked cruise sign-up sheet. "Someone posted a sign-up sheet." I held it out for her to read.

Her eyes went wide. "Oh, no. This can't happen."

"I agree. It's inappropriate and people will complain."

Jenny started to giggle, then pulled me aside. "Can you imagine how much aloe I'd need to treat all those sunburned wrinkled bodies?"

"That's your first thought? Aloe for sunburn?"

She laughed and her tummy bounced. "Actually, my first thought was how...unattractive all those sagging senior bodies would be. I've seen many of them and..."

I put up my hand and shook my head, trying to banish the image. "Well, don't worry because it's not going to happen."

* * *

The morning flew by as residents stopped off, one at a time, in twos, and in larger groups, to discuss our in-house Buccaneer Days events. At noon, Jenny stepped into my office and held out a paper lunch sack.

"What's this?"

"I made myself a tuna sandwich for lunch. When I took it out of the refrigerator the smell made me a little nauseous."

I removed the plastic bag and was about to unzip it when Jenny put up her hand and turned her head. "What?"

"I told you, the smell is making me nauseous. If you open it, I'll probably throw up."

I set the bag aside. "I thought you were past morning sickness."

"I am, but there are still smells that set me off."

"But you mixed the tuna for the sandwich…"

"That was then. This is now. I can't explain what sets me off, but *that* does." She took a step back. "When you're through eating it, throw the remnants in the outside dumpster and brush your teeth."

"Do you want me to pick up ice cream and pickles on the way home?"

That garnered a glare. "That's an old wives tale. But I would like some strawberry ice cream." She took half a step and paused. "Am I riding with you to Len's party?"

I almost flipped over turning to see the wall clock. Then I relaxed. "It's not for another two hours."

Jenny nodded. "You'd forgotten."

"No, I just lost track of time." Then I had another panic attack. "Did you buy a gift from us?"

"Of course I did."

"What?" I asked as she retreated.

"You'll be surprised."

I ate the sandwich while studying the Catalina website, advertising the 30th Buccaneer Days celebration. I flipped back to earlier years and the website didn't change a lot except for the dates and the bands playing. I clicked on some of the links and saw pictures of the winning costumes from several years, wenches in various costumes, varying from sedate to revealing, lists of the winning pirate jokes, and video taken as the last Saturday night band played. I leaned back, watching the drunken pirates and wenches gyrating to the music.

"What's that?"

I turned to Dolores, my former neighbor who was now a Whistling Pines resident. "There's a Buccaneers Day celebration in California. This video was taken last year."

Dolores, whose eyesight wasn't great, stepped into my office and leaned over my shoulder. "I'm no prude, but some of those women aren't wearing a lot."

"I think they might've been wearing more clothing earlier in the day, before their blood alcohol got as high."

Dolores continued to stare at the screen, mesmerized by the dancing crowd. "I hope our festival is that well attended. The town could use the tourism boost." She straightened up, holding my chair to steady herself. "Are you wearing the costume in the basement?"

"What costume in which basement?"

"My basement, now your basement."

"There's a costume in the basement?"

Dolores pointed to the screen. "It looks a lot like some of those pirate costumes."

"Why did you have a pirate costume in your basement? Was it from a costume party?"

"Well," she said, sitting in my guest chair, "it wasn't intended to be a costume, but my husband did wear it to a costume ball one year."

"What was it intended to be?"

"It's my father-in-law's Freemason outfit."

"I'm afraid you've lost me."

Dolores let out a sigh. "My father-in-law was the grand royal vizier, or some such title, of the regional Masons and Shriners. He owned a fancy ceremonial uniform from the 1930s. My husband removed the Masonic emblems and wore it as a pirate's costume."

"A Masonic ceremonial uniform looked like a pirate costume?"

"It has a long double-breasted black coat, an admiral's hat with an ostrich plume, a belt and shoulder strap, medals, and a sword."

"And that's all in the basement?"

Dolores got up. "Yes, in a steamer trunk. And now, it's yours." She took a step toward the door, then turned. "Um, you might want to be careful. I think there's an old muzzle-loading pistol in the trunk, and it might still be loaded."

"What?"

"Don't worry. There's probably not a cap on the firing nipple. At least I hope not."

I leaned back and stared at the ceiling. Yet another hidden antique gun, and it *might* be loaded. I try to restrain myself from swearing, instead relying on the perfectly good adjectives and adverbs I've learned over the years. The thought of another loaded gun in the house, even if it's hidden in a trunk, pushed me to the edge. I was about to slam the door and let loose with a tirade when the director stepped in, catching me with my lips forming the profanity that was about to fly out of my mouth.

"Were you leaving?"

I bit my tongue and offered her my visitor chair. "No, I stubbed my toe."

She smiled, apparently cognizant of what I'd been ready to say. "Thanks for helping Meg. She called and said you were polite and gracious. I appreciate what great Whistling Pines ambassadors you and Jenny have become."

"Wendy too," I offered.

Nancy hesitated. "Yes, Wendy often puts us in a good light." Left unsaid was mentioning the times Wendy's antics embarrassed Nancy and left her to patch up the distaste Wendy's often overt frankness left with people.

"Is there something more?"

Nancy swung my office door shut and leaned close. "Let's brainstorm some way to get the interested residents on a birdwatching cruise without putting them on a boat with the nudists."

I choked. "Um, did Jenny mention the shortage of aloe that might result?"

Nancy shook her head. "No, but that's certainly a consideration. There's an awful lot of white skin around here that hasn't seen the light of day in decades. Please set up another option for our residents."

"I'll call the charter office at the Knife River Marina. I'm sure some captain would be willing to take out a group of residents for a nominal fee."

Nancy stood. "Thank you."

Before Nancy could open the door there was a knock. She opened the door and Hulda Packer was standing there, blocking the doorframe with her walker, a charge card in hand. "Oh, Nancy. Hello. I was just going to ask Peter to do one of his Amazon searches for me."

"I'm sure he would be happy to help. What are you shopping for?"

Hulda pushed past Nancy. "I decided to skip the birdwatching. I want a bikini to wear on the nudist cruise. I'm uncomfortable going entirely naked."

A vision flashed through my mind for the briefest second. Some things can't be unseen even if they're only mental images.

Nancy covered her mouth to hide her smile. "I think that's wise."

Hulda and I looked through website after website of bikini-clad young women. After ten minutes Hulda nudged me. "Go to the sites with bikinis for senior citizens."

"I don't think they exist."

Hulda got up. "Fine. If that's your best effort, you've left me tasteless."

Hulda regularly got words confused. I'd learned to smile and try to steer her to the correct word. "I don't think tasteless is the word you're looking for."

"All right, you've disapplied me."

"Disappointed," I corrected.

"That too," she said, stomping out.

I glanced at the last site we'd searched and looked at the bikini model who looked remarkably like Jenny a year ago.

"Ogling strange bikini-clad women?"

I turned and glared at Wendy. "How do you…?"

"Know when to show up to catch you using the computer inappropriately? I am the system administrator and I know what sites everyone views."

I closed the bikini site. "Not that it makes any difference to you, I was helping Hulda Packer try to find a bikini."

Wendy sat in my chair. "I know. I went to a site with senior citizen beachwear and we found one she liked in about seven seconds. If you hadn't spent all your time ogling the pretty young things on those sites for teenagers, you might've found one for her on your own."

I glanced at the clock. "I've got to leave for Len Rentz's retirement party."

Wendy got up. "Meg Cochran invited my band to play for Buccaneer Days. We need a rhythm guitar player who can sing."

"With Jenny very pregnant, my first priority will be keeping track of Jeremy in the crowd. Sorry."

Wendy nodded, and in an unusually touching gesture, put her hand on my shoulder. "I get that. I hope this goes well for all of you. Jeremy's got to be struggling."

"He's getting his head around it, but we're not out of the woods yet."

Breaking the moment, Wendy patted my shoulder. "I don't babysit. Don't even ask."

* * *

Mild swells in the protected Knife River Marina caused the sailboats to rock, their hardware clanking in the rigging. Art West's boat had a short somewhere in the marine-band radio circuit. After hours of tracing and testing wires hidden under counters and behind panels, he'd found a spot where the insulation had worn away, shorting the circuit against a metal bracket. With his head under a panel, he sensed the change in the boat's motion as someone stepped aboard.

"I found the problem. It was just a bit of worn insulation causing a short."

Footsteps crossed the deck and Art saw dock shoes coming down the ladder into the cabin. "It was a bugger. Could you cut me a piece of electrical tape from the roll on the table? Just a short bit, maybe an inch long."

There was a hiss, an explosion, and Art felt a white-hot pain in his chest. He was surrounded by smoke, and his first thought was that he'd started an electrical fire and a hot ember fell on him. Then the acrid smell of burned sulfurous black powder filled his nose and his breath caught. He exhaled, bubbling blood filling his mouth. His brain failed to register the sound of footsteps retreating across the deck as his last brain cells shut down, robbed of oxygen when his heart had been pierced by the half-inch diameter musket ball.

Chapter Four

I drove to Judy's with Jenny squirming in her seat, constantly readjusting the seatbelt. "Have you considered getting a different car after the baby's born?" She asked.

The question lost me. "What? Why?"

"We'll need rear-facing infant seats in both of our vehicles and..." she glanced at my backseat, "there's no room for a car seat, plus Jeremy, and your stuff back there."

"I'll put my 'stuff' in the trunk." That stuff being primarily workout clothing and shoes for when I got the chance to exercise or play a pick-up basketball game in the high school gym.

"Let's face it, we've become soccer parents and there's a minivan in your future."

"Why do I have to get the minivan?" I asked.

"Because my car is big enough for a car seat."

Jenny's voice was rising in pitch and in volume. I knew it was time to de-escalate the discussion. "Do you care what brand minivan we buy?"

Jenny relaxed. "Not really, as long as we can get Jeremy, the baby, a baby bag, and sports equipment into it."

I didn't want to vehicle shop on the eve of Buccaneer Days, but I knew it was time to throw in the towel, even if I didn't plan on following through for several weeks...or months. "I'll look into it."

I knew better than to use the parking lot, having learned that pregnant Jenny needed more space to get in and out of the car than pre-pregnancy Jenny. Finding a street parking spot just past Judy's café, I parked, then helped Jenny out of the car. As we walked toward Judy's, a woman watched us approach while holding an animated discussion with someone on her cellphone. She held the door for Jenny to enter without missing a beat, then ended the call.

"You're Peter Rogers, right?" she asked before I passed.

I nodded, recognizing her face, but not being able to connect her with a specific place or event. Part of living in a small town is seeing everyone at least once or twice a year, always nodding and saying hello, but having only a few people who you connect with. "I'm afraid I'm at a disadvantage."

She put out her hand. "We spoke on the phone. I'm Meg Cochran, the chamber of commerce president."

The pieces came together in my mind. She owned the antiques shop just down the street from Judy's. Len Rentz told me Meg was a force of nature, which made her the perfect person to be president of the chamber. "It's nice to put a face to your name. How did you recognize me?"

"You were the piccolo player at the concert when the crazy woman tried to kill the bassoon player."

"I was a little distracted that evening."

Meg's laugh was as raspy as her voice. "I can imagine, with gunshots flying and your neighbor pulling that old blunderbuss out from under her afghan." Meg stepped back and let a couple pass us and enter Judy's "Do you have any more thoughts about Buccaneer Days?"

"Sorry, I've been busy." A thought popped to mind. "Have you spoken with any of the local fraternal groups? The Rotary club puts on a breakfast every summer, and the Sons of Norway host a big picnic."

"That's a good suggestion. I'll make some calls. I already have several musical groups lined up to play before the big city band concert. I think you know Wendy from the Gin Fizzes. They're going to perform two sets. Then, The Parrot Heads will be performing Jimmy Buffett music."

I ran through Jimmy Buffett's songbook in my mind and smiled.

"What's so funny?"

"I'm picturing a crowd of drunken pirates singing Jimmy Buffett songs."

"What about them?"

"The song *Fruitcakes* talks about strutting down the crosswalk naked in the middle of the week."

Meg looked stunned. "I'll ask them not to sing that song."

"A quarter of Buffett's songs mention or promote drinking. *Margaritaville.*"

Meg waved off my concerns. "I'm sure it'll be okay. I've got Doctor Kielbasa to warm up the crowd for the city band."

"Who or what is Doctor Kielbasa?"

"They're a polka group from Sturgeon Lake. We're really lucky to get them because they're regionally famous. They have two trumpet players, two accordions, a drummer, and a tuba. I convinced them to cut their fee by arguing that their concert exposure will probably double the number of weddings and other gigs they'll book next year." Meg glanced in the Judy's front window. "We'd better get inside before all the pies are gone."

Jenny was sitting at a table near the door with her feet on a chair. "You saved me a spot," I said.

"I put my feet up because they were starting to swell. Find your own chair." I looked around the crowd and realized Jenny had done well to find herself two chairs.

The mayor stood and clanked a spoon on his water glass, bringing silence to the room. "We're here to honor Len Rentz, who's announced his retirement. I know he's been a fixture in the Two Harbors community for a long time and many of you have fond memories of Len's service. Others of you

45

remember him because of your DWI citations." The mayor paused to let the laughter die down. I saw two red-faced attendees who apparently took the DWI comment personally. "I'd planned to give Len a gold watch until I found out how much they cost. Instead, I'm offering Len a hearty handshake and wishing him well."

Len stood, looking uncomfortable as the laughter died. He wore a plaid shirt instead of his uniform, the transformation making him look shorter and older. He waved at the crowd as they clapped. When the applause stopped, he cleared his throat. "My dad always said the best sermons and speeches were short. Thanks for coming. Have more pie."

The mayor was caught by surprise by Len's short speech and struggled to his feet. "If there's anyone else who has something…"

I felt a pain in my shin and looked down just as Jenny kicked me a second time. She held out a wrapped package and nodded toward the head table. I wound through the tables as people turned to stare. Finally getting to Len I turned to the crowd. "Len has been like a father to me and got me through some rough patches. I just wanted to say…" then my voice broke and I handed him the box.

He stood again, nodding his thanks. He ripped the paper away and stood staring at the shadowbox in his hands. Tears filled his eyes and rolled down his cheeks. He looked at me and mouthed, "Jenny." I nodded.

Someone in the back yelled, "What is it?"

Len held the gift high, turning it so everyone in the small café could see the shadow box Jenny made. The box held the brass nameplate from his uniform, a Two Harbors Police shoulder patch, a set of sergeant's stripes, his gold badge, and the gold chief's stars from his uniform collar.

He handed the box to me and said, "Hold this," then he pushed through the crowd until he got to Jenny where he got on his knees to hug her.

There was hardly a dry eye in the café when the mayor stood. "In case you haven't met the new chief, his name is Kerry Stone." Another round of applause rippled through the small space. "Well, it appears we've run Judy out of pie. I'm buying the first round of drinks at the VFW."

Kerry jumped on a chair and shushed the crowd. "Just to be clear, free drinks to celebrate Len's retirement doesn't mean the DWI laws are suspended. I'll be at the door collecting keys from anyone who shouldn't be driving themselves home!" He looked at me. "Since it appears I might be collecting a lot of keys, Peter, do you think you could borrow the Whistling Pines van and provide sober cab service this evening?"

I glanced at Jenny, who released Len's embrace. She nodded. "I think that can be arranged."

* * *

After spending an evening at Len's second retirement party, I transitioned from club soda to sober cab driver. As the second load of revelers handed their keys to Kerry, the new police chief pulled me aside while the passengers loaded into the Whistling Pines van.

"Thanks for doing this. I really didn't want to be writing a bunch of DWI citations my first day as chief."

I watched Wilbur Picket, who was on the waiting list for a Whistling Pines opening, trip on the bottom step and sprawl into the van. "I think writing DWIs might've been the least of your worries. I suspect you might've responded to a rash of accidents, hoping none of them were serious."

Kerry blew out a breath and pushed his cap back with a badly scarred hand, a remnant of the Iraq IED that caused a fire, disfiguring his face and hand. I chose not to dwell on the scars hidden under his shirt or the ones in his mind. "What do you know about this Buccaneer Days festival?"

"I know it started with tourists finding a Two Harbors California website and mistaking it for here. They started booking rooms, expecting a party. The motels called Meg Cochran looking for information to pass along to the guests. Meg, seeing a chance for the local businesses to make some sorely needed tourism dollars during our few weeks of summer, started calling the chamber of commerce members and selling them on the idea of having our own Buccaneer Days. I guess if you wanted more background, you should start with the California website to see what they're doing. Meg wants to mirror their festival so the town can leverage the tourists who've confused us with the other Two Harbors."

Kerry looked down the street at a couple walking home from the VFW arm in arm. "I looked at that website. It scared the hell out of me."

"How so?"

"It's filled with photos of people dressed like pirates drinking and doing stupid things. I got forwarded to a YouTube video of two men having a mock cutlass battle in the street."

"I'm sure they were using plastic swords."

Kerry looked at me. "Their swords clanked when they struck each other. They were not plastic."

"I'm sure they were dull, like the swords people carry at renaissance festivals."

Shouts echoed inside the VFW and Kerry stepped toward the door. "How will we know which swords are sharp or dull?"

It was after midnight before I got home. The bedroom light was on and Jenny was pacing the bedroom. "What's up?"

"I've had a couple contractions."

My eyes must've gone wide because Jenny sensed my panic and waved it off. "It's not a big deal. There were two, spaced an hour apart, and they've stopped."

"You're not due for two weeks."

Jenny smiled. "I don't suppose delivering babies was part of your Navy corpsman training. Babies come when they want. Jeremy was a week late. His sibling might decide to make an early appearance."

I sat on the bed. "We spent a day talking through the mechanics of delivering a baby, but we never got into the physiology of a pregnancy. Due dates vs. delivery dates never came up. The instructors last words were, 'Now you know how to do this, try never to use this skill. Do whatever you can to get the mother to a hospital before the baby crowns.'"

"That's good advice, but the reality is, we have no control over when, or how fast a baby delivers."

"But…"

Jenny put up her hand. "Women have given birth to babies for thousands of years before there were midwives. Then they used midwives for another half century before there were obstetricians and birthing rooms. Most babies are amazingly resilient. You only need the hospital for the exceptions."

"And to provide drugs."

Jenny smiled. "Having been through this once, I'll gladly accept any pharmaceuticals offered." She paused. "How did the sober cab go?"

"No one threw up inside the van."

"I guess that's something positive. You got everyone home and tucked into bed?"

"I didn't tuck anyone in bed. All I did was make sure they got inside their houses. The rest was up to them."

"Did you get propositioned?"

I must've blushed because Jenny grinned. "Who?"

"Marcella Young invited me in for a nightcap."

Jenny shook her head as she grinned. "Is that why you're so late? You took her up on the offer?"

Marcella was a youngish widow who was known around town as a cougar, looking for a younger man to warm her bed. "I told her I was flattered by her offer, then politely declined."

"Good choice, sailor boy."

I shook my head as I stripped out of my clothes. "Go to bed. I'm going to take a shower, then I'll be right in."

I returned to a dark bedroom and slipped into bed, spooning into Jenny's back.

She pulled my arm across her tummy. "I'd forgotten what misery the third trimester of a pregnancy could be."

"I think that's nature's way of perpetuating the species. You forget about the nine-month pregnancy when you see the cute baby in your arms."

"I've heard the adrenaline and hormones block the memory of the delivery pain, but every woman who's been through pregnancy remembers the physical discomfort, feeling unattractive, and knowing there isn't enough room in her belly for a baby, stomach, and bladder."

"It'll be over soon."

Jenny struggled to roll over, then faced me. "If I ever say I want to have another baby, please remind me of these few weeks."

"Do you want me to have a vasectomy?"

Jenny rolled over and stroked my face gently. Her face was lit by the moonlight shining in the bedroom window. "The Christmas elf left a whole row of stockings to fill the hooks under the fireplace mantel."

I kissed her gently. "Just because we have all those stockings, doesn't mean we need to supply a baby for each of them."

"Let's defer this discussion until next Christmas." The baby squirmed, gently kicking my stomach where it rested against Jenny's abdomen.

Jenny rolled over and pulled my arm over her side. "Did anything else interesting happen tonight?"

"Kerry Stone is nervous about Buccaneer Days."

"As well he should be. It'll be a zoo."

"Let's take a vacation. Maybe a trip to Grand Marais or Thunder Bay for the weekend."

"I'm staying close to the hospital and my obstetrician until the baby arrives."

Chapter Five

The doorbell rang while I was shaving. No one ever used our doorbell except on Halloween or if Jehovah's Witnesses were trying to save our souls. Neither of these came in the morning. I rushed through my shave, nicking my chin, then pulled on a t-shirt and a pair of jeans.

Jenny and Kerry Stone were sipping coffee and chatting at the dining room table while Jeremy shoveled cereal into his mouth while reading the box. I nodded to Kerry and got myself a cup of coffee. I was surprised when Kerry followed me into the kitchen.

"Can I top off your coffee?"

Kerry shook his head and put his cup in the sink. "It's started."

I took a sip of coffee, hoping the caffeine would overcome the tiredness left after five short hours of sleep. I froze when I realized Kerry's eyes were more tired than mine and he was running on even less sleep than I was. "What's started?"

He nodded toward the kitchen door and we stepped onto the back step. He closed the door, and we stared at the dew-covered grass. "A body was found in a sailboat in the Knife River Marina."

"A dead body?"

Kerry pinched the bridge of his nose. "Yes, Peter, the body is dead. If they'd found a live body, I wouldn't be here."

I was barefooted and realized how cold the concrete steps were. "Why *are* you here?"

Kerry stared at his feet for a second, then looked directly into my eyes. "Len trusted you. He told me you were smart and discreet. That, and you've undoubtedly seen more bullet wounds than all the northern Minnesota hospital doctors combined. I'd like you to take a ride with me."

"Where are your cops? Why aren't you taking them with you?"

Kerry turned toward the garage and blew out a breath. "Grif and Shelly are good traffic cops and Daryl is a whiz on the computers. None of them are prepared to investigate a murder. I know you and Len solved a couple murders."

"I have to be at work in an hour."

"Len said your boss was very accommodating."

I stared at the garage. I knew the cops Kerry mentioned. Grif was past retirement age and set in his ways. Shelly and Daryl were inexperienced rookies. "Let me put on a pair of shoes."

"Thanks," Kerry said. Then he added, "You're going to need a fleece too. The boat is docked in the marina and it's cool on the water."

I'd ridden with Len in the unmarked chief's car more often than I cared to admit. Kerry and I chatted about Jeremy and his son, Jacob, who is the same age, his decision to accept the chief's job. His wife was excited about becoming part of a community after bouncing around the country as an Army wife prior to his medical discharge.

Kerry parked between an ambulance and a fire truck. Four firemen, dressed in heavy gear, nodded to him as we passed. The two ambulance attendants nodded from inside the cab where they were keeping warm. Another fireman waited for us in a small motorboat at the end of the dock. He started the outboard and we raced across the marina toward a large sailboat where the harbormaster stood awaiting us, standing on the dock.

Ray Bandeau, a middle-aged former Navy sailor, then commercial fisherman, helped us onto the boat with calloused hands that felt like they'd handled a million ropes. "Chief."

Kerry nodded. "I assume you know Peter Rogers."

Ray nodded. "Peter and I have commiserated over a beer at the VFW. You should join us some time."

"I'm not much of a drinker," Kerry said, handing us plastic gloves.

Ray stopped, blocking the entrance to the sailboat cabin. "Let me be clear, the VFW is more about commiserating with other vets than it is about the beer." He turned and led us to the stairs/ladder. We climbed down to a small galley where a male body lay face-up on the floor with tools spread around him. He was dressed in a blue sweatshirt featuring a picture of the Duluth lift bridge. A dark hole the size of my thumb, was centered in the bridge span. Blood pooled around him on the deck.

Kerry watched me take in the scene. "What do you see?"

"Dead guy. The blood on the deck has mostly dried and his skin shows livor mortis marbling, so he's been dead at least a couple days. The victim's sweatshirt is stippled with burned powder, so the shooter was close when the gun was fired. The single big-bore gunshot wound to the lower chest probably ripped right through the victim's heart. He didn't live long enough to dial 911."

"You couldn't have saved him?"

I glanced away from the body and looked at the bulkhead behind the dead man. "He would've died even if a trauma surgeon had witnessed the shot." I paused. "Who is he?"

"Art West, the boat's owner."

I nodded and looked at Kerry. "I assume you've called the medical examiner?"

"The ambulance crew pronounced the victim dead. The medical examiner suggested getting a Bureau of Criminal Apprehension CSI team here to process the scene. The ME will do a post-mortem exam after the body is delivered to him."

"Have you called the BCA?"

"They're dispatching their regional team, but they won't be here for hours."

"What do you want from me?"

"Tell me about the wound."

Carefully avoiding the blood, I knelt next to the body and looked around. "Well, he wasn't lying here when he was shot." I pointed to a round hole in the woodwork above the countertop. "I'll wager the bullet passed through his body and there's a slug in the wood there. If you carefully dig it out, you'll be able to compare the marks on the bullet to a weapon."

Kerry shook his head. "The hole in the wood is the same size as the entry wound."

I compared the holes. "Interesting. He was shot with a jacketed bullet."

"There won't be any lands and grooves on the bullet. Sniff the air and tell me what you smell."

I sniffed. "I smell lake air with a hint of fish."

"Do you smell the acrid stench of smokeless powder, like after an Iraq firefight?"

I froze, thrown back in time to Iraq. Shots rang in my ears. Shouted orders, then a cry for a corpsman. A Marine was injured and needed my immediate medical attention. Duty and adrenaline overcame fear as I prepared to jump from cover to run through the gunfire.

"Peter?"

Kerry's voice pulled me back from the haunting vision. I was sweating and breathing heavily. He put his hand on my shoulder and whispered, "Stand down, sailor. You're home." He knew exactly what I was going through. He, too, endured nightmares in vivid color with the sounds and smells of the battlefield. The ones that woke your wife when you thrashed in the bed.

"The smell, Peter. What do you smell?"

I sniffed again. "I smell…musty burned matches."

Kerry nodded. "Black powder is made from potassium nitrate, sulfur, and charcoal. You smell the burned sulfur. I'll bet the victim was shot with a muzzle-loader."

"This guy's been dead for a while. Why do we still smell the burned powder?"

Kerry nodded. "The smell was trapped in this enclosed space and has permeated all the cloth and porous material. I bet the cabin was filled with smoke when the gun went off."

"That's insane," I said, standing. "Who carries around a muzzle-loader? It's not even deer hunting season."

"A pirate carries a muzzle-loading pistol."

The harbormaster concealed a grin. "I hate to laugh at a funeral, but maybe you're lucky he wasn't killed by a cutlass. That'd be even harder to match than a pirate's pistol."

Kerry shook his head and blew out a breath. "Buccaneer days have begun."

The paramedics and two firemen were standing on the deck with a body bag and backboard when we climbed out of the sailboat cabin. Kerry nodded to them and they carried the gear into the cabin.

"If we're done, I'm late for work."

Kerry nodded to the harbormaster and we climbed into his small boat. The engine purred as we crossed the marina. Kerry stared at the sailboat. "Ray, did you hear a gunshot?"

Ray shook his head. "Two days ago? I don't think so. I'm not around at night and this is not a quiet place during the day. The sailboat riggings jangle, the boats thump against their bumpers, boats motor in and out, and my hearing isn't that great after years around big diesel engines."

"Do you keep a log of who's in and out of the marina?"

"There's no list. I see some people come and go to the boats with slips. I take people out to their moored boats, but I don't keep a list of them either."

"Do you remember who was around two days ago?"

Ray chuckled as he eased the boat against the pier's rubber bumpers. "My memory is in the same category as my hearing."

"Did you take anyone to the boat where Mr. West was killed?" I asked.

"Not besides Art. But all the larger boats have dinghies or rafts. I wouldn't have noticed anyone motoring around the marina unless they were being unsafe or looked suspicious." Ray paused, deep in thought. "There might've been someone out there. A couple of dinghies came into the pier. One picked up a grocery delivery. I remember them loading bags from a pickup into the boat. There were a couple others I glanced at but didn't take any special notice."

Kerry frowned. "As harbormaster, I'd expect you to keep closer tabs on what's going on."

Ray took out a tissue and wiped his nose, obviously stalling. "People pay big bucks to moor their boats here and they expect...discretion. Some younger folks come out with a case of beer. The guys get together to play cards. A captain has a visitor he doesn't want the people in town to see. I turn a blind eye unless they're stealing or damaging something."

"So, you've conveniently forgotten if some boat owners were underaged drinkers or illicit visitors." Kerry paused, but Ray didn't respond. "If you remember names of anyone who was around, please call me. I'd like to ask them if they heard a shot or noticed anything suspicious."

Ray smiled. "I remember one person. He has a solid alibi."

Kerry cocked his head. "What's his alibi?"

"He was in his boat all afternoon with the girlfriend his wife doesn't know about."

"Why would you remember his visitor and not others?" I asked.

"He might be a couple months behind on his fees. I'm less enthusiastic about his privacy than the people who pay on time."

Kerry took out a pen and notebook. "The name?"

"Slick Hayes."

"Do you have his phone number?"

Kerry didn't recognize the name, but I knew it and spoke up. "You can get it off any of the billboards advertising his insurance agency. Everyone in town knows him as Slick, but his name is Malcolm."

Kerry put his notebook away, shaking his head. "He's our insurance agent."

Ray nodded down the shoreline. "You don't have to call. He's on the boat now. First pier, third slip on the right."

We watched Kerry walk toward the pier when I had a sudden thought. "Is he alone on the boat?"

Ray grinned. "He likes to come out during the week with his girlfriend."

"Malcolm is married, right?"

Ray glanced at me. "He is."

"You should've warned Kerry."

Ray shook his head. "I've warned Slick that the piers aren't private. It'll serve him right."

"The boats are private."

Ray nodded as Kerry walked the pier. "They are, but that doesn't mean people won't notice the boat rocking or hear noises from the cabin as they pass. Several people suggested he sound-proof the forward berth."

"What's boating etiquette for boarding someone's boat in a slip?"

"If no one's on the deck, most people step on and announce themselves. Then, they wait until someone comes up from the cabin or invites them into the cabin."

Kerry stepped onto the boat and stepped to the cabin door. We couldn't hear if he'd announced himself over the sound of the motorboat approaching with the shooting victim. Kerry opened the cabin door and stepped inside. He was out almost immediately, moving more quickly than when he'd approached.

"Slick's wife doesn't notice there's been another woman on board?" I asked.

"His wife gets seasick. She likes to keep the horizon in view and rarely leaves the deck."

Kerry glared at Ray as he approached. Ray just smiled. "Short interview, chief."

"You could've warned me he had company."

Ray looked past Kerry as Malcolm came out of the cabin tucking his shirttails into his jeans. "How would I know he had company?"

Kerry's smile was lopsided because of the burn scars on one side of his face. "I assume he arrived with the girl."

Ray shook his head. "No. He came by himself."

"And you didn't see the woman go to his boat?"

"She walked past. I didn't see where she went."

Malcolm trotted toward us as we watched in silence. I whispered to Kerry as he neared, "I assume they were practicing for the nudist cruise."

Kerry turned to me slowly and closed his eyes. "I already hate Buccaneer Days."

Ray's laughter turned into a coughing fit as he walked back to his office.

Malcolm was amazingly composed. "Congratulations, chief. First day on the new job?"

"And it's already memorable."

Malcolm froze when he saw the men lifting the body bag out of the boat. "Uh oh. A drowning?"

"Were you on your boat two days ago, Malcolm?"

"Yeah, I was...polishing the brass."

A blonde peeked out of Malcolm's cabin, trying to look nonchalant. "Is that what you call it?"

Malcolm shrugged. "Why?"

"Did you hear a gunshot?"

Malcolm looked at the body bag and made the connection. "Um, no. I didn't hear anything but the usual marina noises."

"When were you onboard?"

"Noonish until maybe one."

Kerry waved to the blonde who was trying not to make eye contact with us. Finally acknowledging his waves, she approached us. "What's up, chief?"

I didn't recognize her, but she seemed to know Kerry. "Did you hear a gunshot when you were here two days ago, Patty?"

"I wasn't..." Patty looked at Malcolm who shook his head. "Um, no. I didn't hear a gunshot."

"When were you on the sailboat?"

"I came down after I got off for lunch, so a little after noon. I have to be back by one."

"Thanks."

Patty was nervous. "Um, chief, you don't need to mention this to Deb, do you?"

Kerry shook his head. "I don't discuss police business at home."

Patty looked relieved. "I don't usually do this with married men." Then she hurried away.

Kerry watched her walk away. "She doesn't usually do this with married men? Does that mean she does it more often with single or divorced men?"

I put up my hands. "I have no idea."

"Either way, they're not breaking any laws."

"Do you know Patty?" I asked.

"She's a neighbor."

"A married neighbor?"

Kerry looked at Malcolm, then back at me. "Not currently. But she has two kids in daycare."

We both looked at Malcolm's smile. "You've got to love a small town, eh?"

I followed Kerry to the harbormaster's shed. "I suppose you need to notify the next of kin."

Kerry stopped. "Me?"

"You're the police chief."

"Doesn't the sheriff do that?"

"Len always did the notifications for deaths in the city."

Kerry looked resigned. "I assume the harbormaster has the victim's address."

The harbormaster pulled up Ray West's address on his computer and printed a copy for Kerry. "His wife's name is Colleen."

Kerry folded the address and put it in his pocket. "Does she sail with him?"

"She's the one who wanted to buy the boat. He's a reluctant sailor at best."

Kerry leaned on the counter, looking earnest. "Is there anything else we should know about the victim?"

The harbormaster's eyes narrowed. "Like what?"

"Does he bring down visitors like Malcolm?"

"No, not like Slick."

"You hesitated. Why?"

The harbormaster shrugged. "No reason."

"He's dead, you don't need to protect his privacy."

Ray pulled a pack of nicotine gum out of his pocket and popped one in his mouth. "Smoking will kill you, but this stupid gum isn't as satisfying as a cigarette."

"You're evading my question."

Ray's eyes narrowed. "Colleen was a sailor, like she was one with the boat. Art was learning, but his biggest contribution was fixing things when they broke."

"It looked like he was fixing something when he was killed."

"Yeah, Colleen said something about the marine radio shorting out when she came in Monday. Art was probably fixing it."

"Were they party people or heavy drinkers?"

Ray looked out of the window overlooking the marina. "I never saw them bringing a lot of booze onboard or a bunch of people. They were more serious sailors. They entered the regattas and gave the best of the fleet a run for their money."

"Colleen captained?"

"Colleen was at the helm when they won."

Kerry made notes. "And Art was along as crew."

"Sometimes Art, sometimes other people were her crew."

"Focus on the victim's boat. Who have you seen coming and going?"

"His friends. Her friends. Their friends. Others I don't know."

"And what's going on?"

"I never see anything happening on deck, if that's what you're asking."

"But you suspect more might be going on inside the cabin."

"There's a marina saying, 'What happens on the boat, stays on the boat.' Nobody comes in here telling tales."

"What do you suspect? Drugs? Sex? Something else?"

"Listen, Wests are nice folks. They pay their mooring fee on time. They take their boat in and out of the marina without banging into other boats and they're good sailors. Their boat passes Coast Guard inspections. They don't host noisy parties in the marina.

They send me a Christmas present. I've got no complaints."

"But someone was unhappy with Art."

"I couldn't tell you who it would be. He was a nice guy."

Kerry was deep in thought as we walked to his car. "It's interesting that the wife is the sailor. She's the only female captain I know."

* * *

Kerry turned left out of the marina. "You turned the wrong way. I need to get back to work."

"Hang in there with me. I don't want to visit a bereaved widow alone."

"I don't want to tell a woman her husband died. It's not my job."

"You could get out of the car and walk back to work." Kerry smiled. "Or call a taxi."

I glanced at the speedometer. "I'm not getting out at fifty-five miles an hour."

West's driveway was opposite the lake, winding up a hillside. We curled around a switchback and rose up in front of a two-story house with a brick façade. Kerry parked on the concrete apron in front of the steps.

I followed him to the door. "I don't want to do this."

"Shh."

Colleen West was attractive with sandy hair pulled into a bun. Her freckles were enhanced by her exposure to the sun. I guessed she was thirty. A look at her hands told me she was closer to fifty, having suffered a lot of sun damage. I'd seen her shopping in town and has been struck by her natural beauty. She never wore makeup and didn't need it to turn heads.

The sight of Kerry's uniform caught her off guard. "Can I help you?"

Kerry removed his cap. "Are you Colleen West."

The question put her on edge. "Yes, what's this about."

"I'm Chief Stone and this is Peter Rogers. May we come in for a minute?"

She hesitated for a moment, then stepped back, holding the door for us.

West's house was relatively new, built into the rocky hillside. Colleen gestured for us to go into her living room. The entire east wall was windows overlooking Lake Superior. Every piece of furniture was arranged with a view of the lake and the walls were covered with framed Craig Blacklock photos of the lake, taken in different seasons of the year.

We sat on the couch with Colleen sitting on the edge of a chair to the side. Her anxiety was palpable. "What's going on, Chief Stone?"

Kerry took a deep breath. "Your husband was killed on your sailboat."

Colleen took a quick intake of air, followed by a gasp. "Killed?" she asked as tears filled her eyes. "I don't understand."

"When did you see him last?"

"Um…he went down to work on the boat Tuesday morning."

"You weren't surprised when he didn't come home?"

Colleen wiped her eyes with a tissue, then shook her head. "He sometimes spends the night on the boat when he's in the middle of a project."

"That was two nights ago."

Colleen nodded. "There was an electrical problem. He texted me Tuesday afternoon saying it might take a while to trace and repair it. I thought…"

Kerry took out a notebook and pen. "Do you know anyone who'd harm your husband?"

"I…" Colleen leaned back in the chair. The words stuck in her throat.

The situation finally got to her, and she burst into tears. She pulled her feet under herself and curled into a ball. Sobs wracked her as we sat watching. I felt out of place, intruding on this terrible, personal moment. I glanced at Terry who was writing notes in his pad. His breathing was shallow, and he too was trying to stay composed, his emotions barely under the surface.

After a few moments Colleen looked up, seeming almost surprised to see us still there. "I'm...sorry. Um...what happened? You said Art was killed on the boat?"

Kerry clutched his notebook. "He was shot in the sailboat cabin."

"Why? Did someone steal his wallet or...?"

"Where have you been the last two days?"

The question caught Colleen off guard. "Me?"

"I'm sorry, but I need to ask."

"Um...here. I work from home. I was logged onto the computer and..." She paused. "Why are you asking where I was?"

"I'm sorry, but I have to tie down the timeline."

Colleen became agitated. "I didn't kill him. He's my husband. I love him...loved him."

Kerry nodded. I felt embarrassed, but he was confident and firm. I was struck by his professionalism. Kerry was good. He deserved the chief's job.

"Do you know anyone who wanted to harm Art?"

Colleen shook her head. "He didn't...we...aren't violent people. I mean, we're computer people. It's not like we make trouble. No one gets mad a programmers. We just do...computer stuff."

"How about at the marina? Is there anyone who was mad about something going on with the boats?"

Colleen was speechless. "Something with the boats? I don't understand?"

"Was anyone mad because something happened with the sailboat?"

"We're weekend sailors and..." Colleen paused. "We're very competitive when we're racing, but no one gets mad. We race, then congratulate the winner and go out for dinner together."

"You haven't bumped someone's boat in the marina or argued over where you're docked?"

"No. Never."

Kerry folded up his notebook and we stood. "I'm very sorry for your loss, Mrs. West. I apologize for the questions, but I need to know where to investigate."

Colleen followed us to the door and we stopped on the top step. "Do you sail a lot, Mrs. West?"

"We're on the water every chance we get." She paused. "You know how it is up here. The sailing season is only four or five months and the lake is too rough half those days. We like to take the boat out whenever we get a sailing day. My work is flexible, so I often go out during the week when everyone else has to be at a job. It is...was magical to go out when I'm in the only boat out of the marina. It's like I have the whole lake to myself."

Kerry handed her one of Len's cards. He'd crossed out Len's name and written his in its place, with a handwritten cellphone number. "Thanks. If you think of anything, please call."

Colleen fingered the card and nodded.

* * *

"What do you think?" Kerry asked as he pulled onto Highway 61.

"What do I think about what?"

"Colleen and her reaction to the news."

"I don't know. She seemed upset."

"Art died two days ago and she didn't seem concerned that she hadn't heard from him since his Tuesday text."

"She said he stays on the boat when he's working on it."

"How concerned would Jenny be if she hadn't heard from you in two days?"

"It's not the same thing. We're newlyweds with a kid. We work regular jobs and have structure to our lives. Colleen and Art work from home and seem...independent. Besides, why would she kill him?"

Kerry focused on the road. "Love and money are the two biggest murder motives."

"Can you picture her walking up to Art and shooting him in the chest with a muzzle-loading pistol?" I paused. "I can't. I think it was something related to the boats and someone is using Buccaneer Days to cover

74

up whatever motive they've got for killing Art."

"One of the men dressed up like a pirate?"

I nodded. "Half the people in town will be dressed like pirates. There will be fifty guys wandering around town with swords and pistols this weekend."

"Most of them will be tourists, Peter, and none of them killed Art. This was personal. Someone who knew him wanted him dead."

"Have you ever investigated a domestic assault where a wife shot her husband?"

"Only once. He'd beaten her badly and she'd wrestled the gun away from her husband when he was threatening to kill her."

"Colleen didn't look like a battered wife."

Kerry thought as we passed through town. "No, she's confident and professional. She doesn't fit the psychological profile of a battered spouse."

"It wasn't a robbery. Art's wallet was still in his pocket."

Kerry shook his head. "So a pirate walks onto the boat, pulls his pistol, and shoots a guy."

"That sounds like the opening line of a joke."

Kerry snorted. "I wish I knew the punchline.

I looked at one of Malcolm's billboards on the corner where Kerry turned toward

Whistling Pines. "Our insurance agent is a busy guy. In addition to his service, it seems like he likes to spread his pollen."

Kerry glanced at me. "I was referring to the murder."

"The harbormaster told us people were coming and going but he couldn't identify any of them. He didn't really give you anything to work with except someone took groceries to their boat."

Kerry nodded. "I plan to track them down. Anything else that jumps out at you?"

"You could get a list of the boat owners and call them."

Kerry blew out a breath. "I'll ask our clerk to start calling. She can narrow the list to the people who were there Tuesday."

"That'll help, but you won't get the names of the people, like Malcom, who don't want to admit they were on their boats."

"It's too bad there's not a camera overlooking the marina. Any other ideas?"

"Nope, I'm out of thoughts." I looked at Kerry. "You're an experienced investigator."

"The primary role of a good investigator is gathering information from reliable sources and I'm neither a resource, nor reliable."

"Come on, Peter. You're smart and intuitive."

"Who told you that lie?"

"Len and everyone else I've spoken with."

I frowned. "You've spoken to a lot of people about me?"

"I don't want Jacob hanging around with some sleazeball's kid. I've got a lot of background on you, and it's all good. You're squeaky clean. I can't even find a record of you getting a speeding ticket." I was still mulling that when Kerry asked, "How's Jenny doing?"

"She's handling the pregnancy better than me. She's uncomfortable, but she's been through it. I'm the one struggling. I didn't anticipate her discomfort, and the mood swings have me ducking for cover."

* * *

Kerry was deep in thought on our return trip to Whistling Pines. He stopped under the portico but didn't unlock my door. "Do you think Art ferried someone out to the boat?"

"It looks to me like he was alone, working on his boat. If he'd brought someone out, there'd probably be some evidence of them, like they were having a beer together or...maybe the sheets in the forward berth would be messed up and stained."

Kerry stared ahead with his hands on the steering wheel. "So, someone motors over to his sailboat, climbs aboard, and shoots him."

"Without any sign of a struggle," I added.

"It was someone he knew, or he was surprised."

"It's hard to surprise someone on a sailboat. He would've heard the motor approaching and felt the motorboat bump into his hull. The boat would've shifted when the murderer stepped aboard. Even if he was deep into his project and missed all those things, he would've heard and seen them climbing down the ladder into the cabin."

Kerry drew a breath and blew it out. "So, the killer was someone he knew."

I shrugged. "That's my take on it."

I hustled back to my office, expecting to see a stack of notes. One yellow note from Jenny sat in the middle of my desk, the only message being a giant question mark. I assumed it related to me being missing during my morning trip with Kerry.

Hustling to the dining room, coffee mug in hand, I threaded my way through the late breakfast crowd. I drew a mug of coffee and surveyed the room as I sipped. My eyes were drawn to a man near the back wearing an eye patch. He was with two other men and they waved me over to their table. It took a second for me to recognize Bill Pierce. I knew he had a glass eye, but I'd never seen him with a black eye patch.

"Peter, I'm getting ready for the costume competition. I bet no one else has a real eye patch!"

I tried not to stare, but the black patch drew my attention. "I've never seen you wear a patch."

Bill leaned back and smiled. "I've owned it for years. I don't wear it because people seem to find my glass eye less obtrusive. I dug it out of my drawer just for the pirate costume party."

Howard Johnson, the self-appointed mayor of Whistling Pines, wore his usual pressed khaki slacks and button-down shirt, showing his military bearing. "Bill and his brother used to play cops and robbers with BB guns until Bobby put a BB in Bill's eye."

Bill shook his head. "That was the end of cops and robbers. My dad took away the BB guns and bent the barrels so we couldn't shoot them anymore. Back in the 50's we never thought much about doing real damage by shooting at each other. I mean, a BB stings when you get hit, but that was part of the fun." He paused and looked out the dining room window at Lake Superior where a pair of fishing boats trolled by. "Yeah, that *Christmas Story* movie with Ralph and his Red Ryder BB gun came about two decades too late to save my eye."

Howard sensed it was time to change the topic. "Peter, I heard you're helping the city plan the big Buccaneer Days celebration."

"I'm more of a consultant. I suggested a couple activities, but the chamber of commerce is the group making all the arrangements."

Howard's sly smile made me uneasy. "I heard the Jolly Rogers are playing at the bandshell."

"They're one of the groups."

Howard nodded. "Does the chamber know they can be a little...salty?"

"Ah, no one's mentioned that."

Howard sipped his coffee to hide his smile. "They should fit right in with the pirate theme."

"Wendy's band is playing, too," I interjected, trying to move before we got into the details of how salty the Jolly Rogers were.

"Wendy mentioned that when she was showing pictures of her wench costume." Howard paused. "She said she needed to buy a couple bottles of sunscreen to make sure she didn't burn skin that wasn't normally exposed to sunlight."

I closed my eyes, trying hard not to imagine how risqué Wendy's costume might be. "I hope she's not planning to wear her costume here."

Bill snorted. "I think we're all kind of looking forward to seeing her costume. I heard we'll see a couple of her tattoos that aren't usually visible."

I looked toward the back corner where Wendy was hunched over a crossword puzzle, oblivious to our conversation across the dining room. I picked up my coffee cup and stood. "I think I'll have to get more details about her costume."

Wendy's pencil was flying from one square to the next and it appeared she was wrapping up the last of the puzzle. She looked up when I stood next to her table. "I've got this one under control. I don't need your help today."

Pulling back a chair, I sat across from her. "There are rumors about your wench costume."

Her eyes lit up and she reached for her back pocket. "Do you want to see a picture of it?"

I put up my hand. "I hope it's appropriate for the workplace."

She slid a picture across the table. "You be the judge."

The elastic-necked peasant blouse was pulled over her shoulders. Coupled with a laced, leather corset, it exposed the Grand Canyon of cleavage along with her bear tattoo and another I'd never seen exposed before. The skirt was designed to look like it was made from rags and a tear over her right leg exposed more thigh than I cared to see. I pushed the picture back. "You can't wear that here. The little old men will have coronaries."

Wendy slid the picture into her back pocket. "Don't worry, I'll slide the top over my shoulders while I'm here and it'll be very discreet."

"And the slit up the thigh?"

"The slit only opens if I pull the fabric aside, like I did in the picture." She paused, and I knew I was going to get needled. "I just hope the elastic doesn't break and cause a wardrobe malfunction. That happened when we were playing a wedding gig at Lutsen and the crowd got an eyeful."

I got up, knowing there was nothing I could say or do that would change Wendy's plans. "Whatever."

Wendy stopped me before I stepped away. "Peter, I know how to dress at work. It'll be fine."

I looked at her and nodded. "Okay."

"Let's do a singalong for the party. I saw the Irish Rovers do a round of *Drunken Sailor* on the internet and they split the crowd in two for the chorus: One half sang, "Way hay." The other half sang, "And up she rises." Then everyone sang, "Early in the morning.""

I had to give Wendy credit, she was creative and made suggestions the residents found fun. "I think everyone would enjoy that."

"Have you ever played a tin whistle?" She referred to a small instrument also known as an Irish flute. I'd learned some songs on a plastic version in sixth grade.

The question caught me off guard. "I owned a plastic instrument they called a flutophone, but I've never played a tin whistle."

"Order one from Amazon. Some pirate songs sound really good with a tin whistle. If you told the band director you could play a tin whistle, I'll bet he'd find a song arrangement that could feature you as a soloist during the Saturday concert."

"That's not a selling point."

Wendy's grin was evil. "I've got John Carr's phone number in my office."

"Don't…"

She was up and gone before I could finish my thought.

A quick internet search on tin whistles soon had me watching songs being played on the instrument. Though thin and metallic the sound had a haunting quality. After watching a civilian piper play *Scotland the Brave* on the tin whistle, I pulled up the bagpipe version. Both were stirring and reminded me of my British/Scottish heritage. I watched a video of the second Scot regiment fresh from Basra Iraq as they marched through cobblestone streets along with six rows of drummers and pipers, all in red coats and kilts. I froze when I realized one of the pipers wore a prosthetic leg below his kilt, a legacy from their Iraq deployment.

Going back to the beginning of the Second Scots video, I watched the rows of soldiers in battle dress, swinging their arms and marching to the beat of the drums. *And each of them has his own nightmares from his time 'in country.'*

I was startled by motion in my peripheral vision. Brian swept into my office and sat in my chair. "What do you call a cow that plays the tuba?"

I shrugged.

"A moo-sician."

"I thought you'd given up tuba jokes for pirate jokes."

"I'm saving my pirate schtick for the joke contest."

"Are the pirate jokes any funnier than the tuba jokes?"

Brian laughed and slapped his leg. "Nothing's funnier than tuba jokes."

I think I moaned, but it might not have been out loud.

"Are you planning to take up the bagpipe too?"

I shut down the Scottish video and turned to him. "I think the neighbors would complain."

"They get used to it. I used to get comments about my tuba practice, but now the neighbors just close the windows. No one calls the police unless the accordion player comes over to practice with me."

"Did you have something special or did you just stop by to tell me the cow joke?"

"I came to tell you about 'Chicken' Jacobs."

"Who's that?"

Brian's eyes gleamed and he leaned forward. "Guess why his nickname was Chicken."

"He lived on a chicken farm?"

"When we were teens, he bragged about playing chicken with the drivers on Highway 61. He'd drive down the wrong lane to see how long it took for the other drivers to steer away."

I glanced at the clock, hoping Brian would catch the hint. "What's that got to do with anything?"

"He's the kind of guy who'd shoot someone on a boat with a muzzle-loading pistol. Did you and the new police chief look to see if there was a bullet hole on the opposite side of the cabin? It might've been a duel."

If Brian's presence wasn't disturbing enough, Hulda Packer pushed her walker through the door. "Sure, it could've been a duel, just like Alexander Graham Bell and Raymond Burr."

That comment caught Brian totally off guard and he looked at me, expecting a reply or correction. "Hulda, it was Aaron Burr and Alexander Hamilton."

"I know that! Weren't you listening just now when I said it?"

I raised my hands in surrender. "How can I help you, Hulda?"

"Would you talk to the kitchen? The doughnuts were greasy, like they hadn't drained them properly. I hate greasy doughnuts. They coat my dentures."

"Did you mention that to the cook?"

"I told everyone in the whole dining room. I expect the cook heard me."

I bet she did, I thought to myself. "Mention it to one of the wait-staff."

"I'm telling you! You have influence here." Hulda pulled her walker back, banging into both sides of the doorframe as she exited.

Brian peeked around the corner to make sure she was gone. "Does that happen often?"

"Do you mean Hulda's confused comments or the complaints?"

"Either. Both."

"Hulda's got a bit of a memory problem. She gets things confused. As for the complaints, they come daily. I pass them along and move on."

"Back to Chicken Jacobs. Like I said, I could see him dueling with someone inside a sailboat cabin."

"Did you mention this to the police chief?"

"I wouldn't bother him with stuff like this."

But it's okay to bother me? "He'd like to know if you have a suspect."

"Chicken's not a suspect."

"You just said…"

"Sure, it's the kind of thing he'd do, but Chicken's dead."

I blew out a breath. "So, why are you telling me about him?"

Brian looked offended. "I thought you'd appreciate the story."

"I suppose he died in a head-on crash and took some innocent soul with him."

Brian stood up. "Oh, no. He died of cirrhosis last year. He liked to play chicken with his drinking buddies, too. I imagine the didn't have to embalm his liver, it was already pickled in alcohol."

I stared at the computer a moment, trying to backtrack and remember my original plans. Failing that, I picked up my coffee cup and walked to the dining room.

* * *

I'd just filled my cup when my cellphone rang. Slopping coffee, I pulled the phone from my pocket, fumbling before I could answer. Setting the coffee cup on a table, I hit the answer button without looking at the caller I.D.

"Peter."

"I just talked to you, Brian."

"I thought of something else. How do you get a million dollars playing the tuba?"

"Aren't you going to save that for your next visit?"

"Naw, I'll have another by then."

"How do you make a million?"

"You start with two million!" Brian cackled. "By the way, the Sons of Norway are working on a boat for the regatta. They've got a yellow and blue sail, and they're fixing up Enos Hagen's sailboat to look like a Viking longboat."

"Brian, why are the Sons of Norway using a sail made in the colors of the Swedish flag?"

"They took a vote and there were more Swedes than Norwegians at the meeting, so they won."

"What's the world coming to when Swedes outnumber Norwegians in the Sons of Norway?"

"I heard they admit anyone who's Scandinavian and keeps their dues paid up. They've even started admitting Finns, who aren't technically Scandinavian." I was reaching for the button to end the call when Brian continued. "I told Meg Cochran they should have a lutefisk throw as part of Buccaneer Days."

I pinched the bridge of my nose. "What's lutefisk got to do with buccaneers?"

"Nothing, but it's always a big draw at the Sons of Norway picnic. There's nothing funnier than watching big bruisers who used to be athletes throwing one-pound hunks of slimy cod. It oozes and breaks into pieces between their fingers."

"I hope Meg said no."

"She's got someone calling around to find lutefisk seconds."

"Huh?"

"You know, grade-B lutefisk. The stuff that's too slimy and stinky to sell as A-one quality."

I'd only eaten lutefisk once and it reminded me of fish flavored gelatin that had been out of the refrigerator too long. "There's some lutefisk that's stinkier and slimier than what's normally served?"

"Oh, yes! I think they feed it to smelling-impaired hogs."

I didn't wait for more. I ended the call.

Howard Johnson, sitting at the table next to me, cleared his throat. "Are you okay?"

I sat next to him. "I just discussed second quality lutefisk."

Howard smiled. "There's no such thing."

"My contact says it's too smelly and slimy to sell for human consumption."

Howard, always composed, bit his lip. "Being a third generation Swede, I don't think there's any lutefisk too disgusting for a bunch of my relatives after two or three rounds of aquavit."

Lefty Christiansen leaned over from the adjacent table. He rolled up his sleeve, exposing a tattoo of a Norwegian flag on his forearm. "Lutefisk is Norwegian comfort food. There's nothing better than a pile of lutefisk swimming in butter gravy. Put it next to a pile of mashed rutabaga and I'd think I'd died and gone to heaven."

Howard was grinning when Lefty turned away. "Is there something I can do for you, Howard?"

"Hulda wants to lodge a complaint about the greasy doughnuts."

"Are you going to tell the cook?"

Howard raised his eyebrows. "Are you kidding? There's no way I'm going to explain how the grease coated Hulda's dentures. I'm just telling you, so you're prepared to hear her whining."

"She mentioned the doughnuts during our discussion of the Alexander Graham Bell and Raymond Burr duel."

Howard tried to look earnest while suppressing a smile. "She told me you were going to recreate it for Buccaneer Days."

I sipped coffee while framing my response. "That's not a pirate thing, so I don't think it's appropriate."

Howard nodded, but his smile worried me. "We'll probably have enough gunfire when the Sons of Norway longboat attacks the regatta with their cannons."

"Attacks the regatta?"

Lefty turned toward us again. "That's what I heard at the Sons of Norway meeting last night."

"I should warn Meg. This is getting out of control."

Lefty waved off my concerns. "No worries. The sailboats in the regatta already know about the Viking ship. I heard some are bringing hoses and are going to douse the Norwegians with bilge water during the attack. I'd feel a little sad for the nudist cruise if they get caught in the middle of the Viking attack."

"There is no nudist cruise. It's Lake Superior and it's always cold, even in the summer."

Arden "Twitch" Larsen rushed into the dining room. He quickly scanned the tables, his left eye tic making it look like he was winking at everyone. Spying Howard, he came to our table.

Spreading the Two Harbors newspaper on the tabletop, he pointed to a circled article. "Can you drive a carload of us into town? The city is sponsoring a medallion hunt and they've put the first clue on this morning's front page."

He pointed to the circled article that announced the medallion hunt and offer of a hundred-dollar prize. The medallion was described as aluminum, with the city logo on one side and an image of a pine tree on the opposite side.

"I talked to a guy who saw one of the city fathers hiding the medallion in the bushes behind Ina Peterson's house last night. You could drive me up there, and I'll grab it and we can collect the prize."

I pointed to the article. "It says right here that the medallion is hidden on public property. It's not in someone's backyard."

"Pfft!" Twitch waved off my comments. "They have to put that in as a red herring. It could be anywhere in town."

I leaned forward. "I talked to the president of the chamber of commerce. The medallion is hidden on public property. They don't want treasure hunters tearing up the whole city."

Twitch frowned. "I still want to check Ina Peterson's bushes."

Lefty, at the next table laughed. "Let me tell you, Twitch. The only thing in Ina's bushes is her neighbor, the window peeper."

Twitch stiffened. "How would you know that?"

"My daughter lives behind Ina, and she called the cops last night when she saw a man peeping in Ina's bedroom window. The cops arrested him."

Twitch was deflated and sat down. "Well, I suppose I'd better re-read the clue."

Search high and low, near and far
On public lands, perhaps near a car
No need for shovels, hoes, or rakes
The entire prize, the winner takes

Twitch studied the clue intently, then pushed the newspaper away. "Bah, this doesn't tell me anything."

Howard put his finger on the poem. "It says near cars, and that you won't need to dig for it."

Twitch shook his head and the tempo of his tic increased. "The town is full of cars and that doesn't mean, you don't have to dig. Where do you hide a medallion without burying it?"

Howard pointed to the first line. "Search high and low. Maybe it's in a tree hollow or under a trash can."

Twitch considered that and nodded. "Archie has a metal detector. I'll get him to bring it along to save us some time."

I cocked my head. "I thought most metal detectors only found iron, copper, or silver."

"Archie's got an expensive one that'll pick up anything. I think it's even got a setting to detect agates."

Twitch gathered the newspaper and left. I looked at Howard. "Agates are rocks. No metal detector will find rocks."

Howard smiled. "Let them have their fantasies."

Lefty turned around and leaned close. "Yah, Archie's metal detector doesn't find agates. That's a myth. Now, Anders Patterson uses a willow divining rod, and he can tune that for anything. The secret is rubbing what he wants to find on the tip before he starts searching. He made a lot of money witching wells, but he's found other things too."

Howard gave me a skeptical glance. "Like what, Lefty?"

Lefty leaned close and whispered. "He's found oil."

"Here?" I asked, too loudly.

"Shh. People don't want other people knowing they've got oil wells on their land."

Lefty turned away and I looked at Howard, who was smiling and shaking his head.

Twitch rushed back into the dining room and sat down. "Dang! The treasure's already been found."

"Where?"

"Ardie Cothern found it in a bottle of pickled herring. It blended right in with the silver herring scales."

Howard failed to cover his snort. Lefty glared at him. "What?"

"Lefty, the supermarket isn't public land and I'm certain the city didn't hide a treasure medallion in a jar of pickled herring in the meat section of the store."

"Well, Mel Rogers told Hulda..."

I put up my hand. "If Hulda told you something, it's almost certainly wrong."

Twitch thought about that, his left eye blinking at me as he pondered my words. "Okay! I'll get Archie and his detector. Howard, will you give us a ride into town?"

"If you buy me a cup of coffee and sweet roll at Judy's."

Twitch considered that for a moment. "A sweet roll and coffee might taste good before we start. It's a deal."

Howard stood and patted my shoulder. "Check your sign-up board."

I got up. "I just took down the fake nudist cruise sign-up sheet."

"I'll wager you that someone replaced it while we talked about lutefisk.

I was walking toward the dining room exit when Margaret Pearson waved to me. Making a U-turn, I walked to the table she shared with three other women and pulled up a chair. "Good morning ladies, what's up?"

Margaret looked around nervously. "I hear you've been investigating my nephew's murder."

The smile melted from my face. "Um, your nephew?"

"Yes, Artie West. He was stabbed on his sailboat."

I closed my eyes and grimaced. As usual, the Whistling Pines rumor mill had a story. They'd gotten part of it right and part of it wrong. I weighed the value of correcting Margaret against acting surprised, or just letting the incorrect information pass.

"Art was your nephew?"

"Yes, he's my sister Christine's son."

"You heard he was dead?"

"The guy who delivered the newspaper told us. He saw them bringing the bloody body from the sailboat when he delivered the harbormaster's newspaper. He said Art was stabbed a couple dozen times by the look of all the blood."

I pictured the bloodless black body bag being handled by the EMTs and shook my head.

"He said you were there with the new police chief, the one who rescued the woman from a fire."

"Huh?"

"Yeah, that's how he got burned, during the rescue."

I sighed. "Chief Stone is a veteran. He was burned during the Iraq war."

"Oh, no. Hulda Packer told us all about the Duluth fire when he saved that woman."

I gave up on correcting the fire story. "Tell me about your nephew, Art."

"He's a nice boy. I always liked him. He's a little odd—never liked to play sports. He was into Legos and building stuff. I think he's an electrician now."

"He's into computer things."

Margaret nodded. "That's what I said. He's an electrician. A computer electrician."

I felt like I was talking with Hulda, who got everything twisted. "Was he well liked?"

"Oh, yes. Everyone liked Artie." Margaret paused. "Well, not everyone. The sports guys used to bully him because he was such a nerd."

"But as an adult, people liked him. He didn't have enemies?" I asked.

"Everyone liked him. He used to fix all their computers and sewing machines. He's really handy."

"So, you don't know why anyone would kill him."

"I can't think of anyone who'd want to hurt Artie. Now, his wife, she's something else."

"His wife, Colleen?"

"Yeah, I used to call her Collie, like the dog, just to irritate her. She moved here from New England." Margaret stopped, deep in thought. "I can't remember which state; I think it was North Carolina. Anyway, she latched onto him and she's just sucking him dry."

"What do you mean?"

"She doesn't work. She just sits around their big house, drinking mimosas, playing computer games, and sailing on their sailboat like she thinks money grows on trees."

"I think she's a computer programmer who works from home."

Margaret frowned. "Works from home! Pfft! She's a lazy one. Who works from home? You can't work from home! You've got to have a job and work somewhere to make money. She just sponged off Artie."

"Artie works from home too."

"Well, that's different. He has a job."

I struggled with the idea that Art could work from home and have a job, but Colleen's work didn't count because she didn't go to a job somewhere. It's a generational thing.

"Collie's a real stinker. She doesn't cook or clean. They hire a maid. We joked that she must be really good in the bedroom, because none of her other housekeeping skills were enough to keep a man satisfied!"

I stood. "Thanks for the input."

Margaret nodded. "You tell the chief that Collie stabbed Artie. She was probably after his insurance money."

I froze. "Art had life insurance?"

"I'm sure he did. He'd need it to pay off that castle they built on the hill south of town. I don't know what they were thinking. They don't have any kids, but they built a house big enough to use as a motel."

"I'll pass that along," I said, suspecting the whole story was a fabrication.

I'd almost exited the dining room when I remembered the conversations about greasy doughnuts. I took a detour into the kitchen. Half a dozen people were either cleaning dishes from the previous meal or preparing food for the next meal.

Opal, the cook, dressed in white with her hair covered by a bouffant hair net looked up from a pan of fish she was breading for the oven. "Peter, get out of here! Your hair isn't covered!"

I held open the dining room door. "Can we talk for a minute?"

Opal was disgusted as she stripped off a pair of gloves and threw them into a waste can. "We're in the middle of meal prep, what do you want?"

"Hulda..."

Opal put up her hand. "Stop right there. I've already heard about the greasy doughnuts. They were just fine. The oil was hot enough and they were golden brown."

"I assumed they were fine, but Hulda asked me to pass along her concern."

"It wasn't a *concern*. It was a *complaint*. You've done your duty. Now, let me get back to the kitchen." I'd turned to leave, but Opal called my name.

"Was there something else?"

Opal's voice softened. "You know my husband, John runs a charter business out of the marina. He heard you were helping the police chief investigate Art West's murder on his boat."

"I'm not helping much."

Opal gave me a dismissive wave. "I know how you used to help Len, but denied you were involved. I assume you're doing the same with the new chief."

"He asked me to go with him to the marina, that's all."

"John's tight with Ray, the harbormaster. There's a lot of fishy stuff going on around there."

I chuckled. "A lot of fishy stuff in the marina. That's a good one."

Opal smiled. "It wasn't meant to be a joke. Ray's trying to keep a lid on things, but some of the sailboat people are getting out of hand."

"What's he concerned about?"

Opal looked around to see if anyone was nearby. "I guess a few of the sailboat people are using their boats to party and entertain. It's getting rowdy on the weekends and they don't mix well with the charter captains who are trying to run businesses."

"I assume the fishing captains are making the harbormaster aware of their concerns."

"Like I said, Ray's trying to deal with it. But, the harbor is his business and he can only go so far without alienating his customers."

"If there's anything illegal going on he should call the police."

Opal sighed. "I think the issues are more nuisance than a legal matter. You know, noisy drunks bothering the people around them."

"Art West's murder is certainly a legal matter." I paused, then had a revelation. "Are you hinting that John, or the harbormaster know something about the murder?"

Opal shook her head. "John would've spoken to the police if he knew something about the murder. But there are a lot of boats in the marina and not all of the captains are as...ethical or responsible."

"What are you trying to tell me? Does John know of someone who's not coming forward with information about the murder?"

Opal put her hands in her pockets. "Casey Bradley didn't have an afternoon charter the day of the murder. He was in the marina at noon and probably spent the afternoon cleaning his boat and prepping it for Wednesday." Opal paused. "Casey's not the kind of person who'd volunteer information to the police. I think he spent some time in prison."

Chapter Six

I took down the hand-made sign-up sheet for the naturist cruise and posted a revised weekly activity schedule that included a pirate singalong and a costume contest. I changed the movie to *Captain Blood,* featuring Erroll Flynn as a doctor turned swashbuckling buccaneer.

Nancy approached me and nodded to a quiet corner behind the aviary. "I heard you turned down John Carr's request that you play with the band."

"I haven't taken the piccolo out of it's case since the last time I played with the band last summer."

Nancy's smile told me I'd already lost the argument. "You'd be playing the same solo as last time. I'm sure it wouldn't take much practice."

"But there's all the other music for the whole concert. I haven't any idea what they're playing, or what instrument they'd want me to play."

Nancy handed me a slip of paper from her pocket. "Here's John Carr's phone number. He can fill you in."

"But..."

Nancy put her hand on my arm. "You're the best ambassador Whistling Pines has. Don't let us down, and don't make me ask again."

I stood with my eyes closed, trying to picture where the piccolo might've been stowed when we unpacked from my small house. I knew where most items were stored, but Jenny and Jeremy helped put things away, and I'd lost control of the unpacking process.

I was startled when Hulda Packer's walker ran over my toe. "Didn't anyone ever teach you to get out of the traffic lane if you're parked?"

I took a step back and gestured for her to pass. She took a step, then stopped in front of me. "Where's the agenda for the bikini cruise."

"Agenda?"

She nodded at the information board, covered with announcements and sign-up sheets. "You know, the agenda we sign to go on outings."

"Ah, the sign-up sheet."

Hulda gave a dismissive wave. "I'd put my name down for the bikini cruise and the sheet is gone."

"There is no bikini cruise."

That got a withering glare. "I ordered a bikini, and I plan to wear it on the boat."

"I don't know if there is a sunbathing cruise, and if there is, it's not something we're involved in."

Hulda clicked her false teeth and snorted. "Well, if you're not going to take us,

I guess I'll have to talk to Wendy. She was signed up, too."

I tried to picture the crumpled piece of paper in my hand without unfolding it to check for Wendy's name. "I guess that's what you'll have to do."

"Some recreation director you are! There's finally something I really want to do, and you put the kibosh on it."

"Do you really want to wear a bikini while cruising frigid Lake Superior?"

"It's not that as much as I want to see all the hard-bodied hunks showing off their twelve-packs."

I closed my eyes. "Twelve-packs are beer can containers. I think you mean six-packs, referring to well-developed abdominal muscles."

Hulda raised her eyebrows. "Maybe I'd like to sample both!"

I stalked into the dining room, hoping to find Wendy working on a crossword puzzle. The one time I wanted to find her, she wasn't in her usual afternoon spot. Miriam, my favorite kitchen person, looked up from making a fresh urn of coffee.

"Are you trying to find Wendy?"

"Yeah, I need to talk to her about the naturist cruise."

Miriam finished her task and wiped her hands. "That's going to be very popular."

"That's the problem, it's not going to happen. I'd rather adjust people's expectations now rather than later."

"You know, half the people who signed up expect to be birdwatching and the other half expect to see naked bodies."

I blew out a breath. "I know, and I fear both groups will be disappointed. Even if there *is* a cruise, people don't sunbathe in the nude when it's fifty degrees."

Miriam nodded. "My husband went out on a charter fishing trip last week. He wore a snowmobile suit and stocking cap."

"Exactly my point!"

Miriam, who always has a way of calming me, pointed to the nearest table. "How are things going with the new family?"

"I think we're adjusting. It's been a little stressful for all of us, but we're getting there."

"Marriage is not for the faint of heart. I assume things improved after you evicted the ghost."

"Yeah, the ghost thing put us all on edge for a couple days. The timing couldn't have been any worse, right after the honeymoon and a week before Christmas."

"I heard about your Christmas present."

I searched my memory, trying to recall anything special I'd received other than wool socks, a winter coat, and a box of chocolate-covered cherries.

"I heard Santa left a row of Christmas stockings for all the hooks under the fireplace mantle. And now Jenny's pregnant, so you've only need four or five more kids to use them all." Miriam got up and patted my shoulder. "You've got some things going for you that most people only dream about."

I nodded. "Getting caught up in the day-to-day battles sometimes makes me lose perspective on the bigger picture. I'm very lucky."

"I heard you're playing piccolo in the city band concert. I hope no one shoots a hole in the tuba like the last time you did the piccolo solo."

I was walking toward the door someone called my name. Three men were sitting at a table near the windows and one waved at me and gestured for me to join them.

I drew another cup of coffee from the urn and sat in the empty chair. "What's up?"

Lars Larson leaned on the table and looked at me earnestly. "Have you heard about Whiskey Row?"

"No. Where is it?"

"Well, it doesn't exist anymore, but it used to be an area north of town where the men lived while the railroad was being built. If you picture the towns in old westerns you'll have an idea of Whiskey Row. It was wooden buildings thrown together and never painted. Of course, the lack of paint didn't mean anything to the guys who lived there."

"I assume it was named Whiskey Row because it was lined with bars."

Skip Hansen nodded. "It was bars, boarding houses, and bordellos. Depending on who you talk to, it was more bordellos than boarding houses. That happens when you've got a bunch of men living without wives around."

"When was this?" I asked.

Marty Winslow looked at Skip and Lars. "I guess it burned down about 1880. A fire started in one part of town and the sparks spread it to everything up there. The university went up there with a bunch of archaeology students in the 1970s and they didn't find much except broken bottles and rusty nails."

I stood up. "Well, thanks for the history lesson."

Lars patted my chair. "We were just getting to the point of the story."

I sat. Like many of the Whistling Pines stories, there had to be a preamble. "What's the point of the story?"

Lars leaned forward like he was going to whisper a secret. "Well, that's where the pirates hung out."

Skip snorted. "There weren't any pirates."

Lars glared at him. "They weren't full-time pirates, like the Caribbean. These guys were opportunists. They didn't have boats or anything like that. Some of them would sneak out and set out lights, so the shore looked like the marina entrance, and hope that a boat would run aground. They'd row out to rescue the crew, then return to loot the ship."

Skip snorted again. "Yeah, and what did your grandpa get when he did that?"

Lars waved his hand dismissively. "Some of the guys got loads of beaver pelts and Canadian whiskey."

Skip leaned forward. "Your grandpa? What did your grandpa get?"

"He was unlucky."

Skip made a gesture for Lars to go on.

"A ship ran aground filled with timber and limestone."

Marty laughed. "So, this ship, the Mary Dresbach, runs aground. They rescue the crew, then go out in the rowboats and the hull is filled with timbers too big to fit in their tiny boats and worthless rocks." Marty paused. "Lars, what happened to your grandpa?"

Lars leaned back and crossed his arms. "The sheriff arrested him and put him in jail for three months. That was the end of his pirate days."

Marty shook his head. "But that wasn't the end. He got out and decided there was money to be made in booze. You've got all these railroad men and Grandpa Larson decided they drink a lot and are probably more interested in the alcohol content than the quality of the booze. So, he set up a still and poured moonshine into the empty booze bottles from the bars, then sold them back to them for half price. Turns out he was wrong about the railroad builders not caring about the quality. A fight broke out in the bar when one of the railroaders thought he'd been poisoned by the bartender and that was the end of Grandpa Larson's bootlegging days."

They looked at me. "How about your family? What did they do?"

I froze. "I don't know much. My grandfather was an engineer on the Burlington Zephyr, between Minneapolis and Chicago."

Lars looked at me for a second. "Those train engineers, they were the cream of society along with the ship captains. They made big bucks in the day."

I slipped away as the conversation returned to Whiskey Row. I wondered how many of the stories were true. *Were there pirates on Lake Superior?*

* * *

Wendy was in the nurse's office sitting on the corner of a desk. She looked up from her conversation with an aide when she saw me. "Peter, did you buy a tin whistle?"

"No, I think the guitar will be enough."

Wendy smirked, knowing I wouldn't jump on her tin whistle idea. "I suppose the residents will have a good time singing sea shanties even if they're only accompanied by guitar. Do you know the guitar chords for *Dead Man's Chest* and *Blow the Man Down*?"

"I'm sure they're out there. Everything's on the internet."

"I think we should be in costume."

I suddenly remembered Dolores' comments about the costume in the trunk and made a mental note to find it. "I'm not sure a pirate's cutlass is compatible with a guitar. I think they'd bang against each other."

Wendy's eye's sparkled and I knew she was about to throw out an idea intended to make me cringe. "Perfect! You play the guitar and I'll swing the sword to the beat of the music."

"It's pointed. You could put someone's eye out."

"I'll stay back from the residents."

"I know. I'm afraid it'll be my eye that gets poked."

"Oh ye, of little faith."

"Oh me, the realist."

Jenny was on the phone, trying to ignore us. She put her hand over the speaker. "Cynic is more like it."

I pointed a finger at her, but she looked away and went back to the phone conversation.

I stalked back to my office, planning to find the guitar chords for pirate songs.

Kerry Stone was sitting in my office visitor's chair, composing a text when I walked in. "Hey, Peter, I've got something for you to look at." He handed me a folder and closed my office door, blocking it with his body.

The folder contained the medical examiner's report along with half a dozen autopsy pictures that I quickly placed facedown on my desk. I scanned the report. "Single wound. The bullet pierced his heart. He died instantly."

Kerry nodded. "Just as you'd observed."

I gathered the pictures and reports and prepared to slide them back into the folder. "Aren't these confidential?"

"Read the medical examiner's comments about the entry wound."

I flipped through the report and studied the ME's observations.

"Particles of burned sulfur and charcoal. The killer was standing close to the victim when he fired. There's black powder residue, as you'd predicted." Kerry accepted the file. "Who brings a black powder pistol on a boat?"

"A pirate?"

Kerry took a breath and let it out. "I don't need a smartass. I need a sounding board who is trustworthy, not a gossip, and who knows police procedures and firearms."

"Sorry."

Kerry sat down without opening the door. "I don't get it. None of the crime scene makes any sense."

"Did you recover the bullet?"

"Yes, it's a tin-lead alloy ball with no barrel marks. It appears to be hand cast by melting the metal, then pouring it into a mold to form the ball. The ratio of tin and lead is the same as plumbers used for soldering copper pipe joints."

"Something that could be purchased at any hardware store or plumbing supply company."

"Actually, there aren't any contractors who use copper anymore. Copper is too expensive and sweating pipes is slow work. The only people who buy solder are repairmen and DIY people rehabbing old houses. I talked to the hardware store. They haven't sold much lately, and they don't keep records on any purchases made with cash or check. Jake, the owner, told me that solder could've been purchased any time in the past decade or more, and anywhere from Canada to Mexico."

"It might be easier to find someone who purchased the dies to cast the bullet or the muzzle-loading pistol."

"I've got Daryl scouring the internet for places that sell antique and replica pistols. I'm not holding my breath. Dozens of internet sites sell replica pistols, and the sale of antique pistols isn't restricted to federally licensed firearms dealers. Anyone can sell and ship an antique muzzleloader. Anyone." Kerry paused. "I got a subpoena for Art and Colleen West's phone records. Art had an incoming call from Colleen's number on Tuesday, as she said. As expected, his phone had no other activity until we found his body. The medical examiner recovered his cellphone with a dead battery before the post-mortem exam."

"And Colleen's phone records?"

Kerry removed a sheet from a sheaf of papers and spread it on his lap. "She uses her phone a lot. I highlighted the call to Art in yellow. There were dozens of calls after that, right up until we showed up at her house to tell her we'd found Art dead. Her first call after that is to a landline in Maine registered to her father. I assume she called her parents to announce Art's death."

"What about the rest of her calls?"

Kerry turned the paper so I could see it. He pointed to a row of blue highlighted calls. "She has hour-long calls to Japan every night. I ran a reverse look-up for the number and it's a video game company."

"Why would she call a game company every night?"

"I had Daryl do an internet search on Colleen's name. Aside from her social networking sites, he found a couple of articles in business magazines about Colleen. It appears she's a gifted game

113

programmer and has patents on some of the most popular interactive computer games."

"She works for someone like Nintendo?"

Kerry shook his head. "Her games are sold as apps for computers and android phones. They're marketed by a Japanese company that I'd never heard of before Daryl showed me the printout."

I looked at the phone call list. "What about the other calls?"

"They're mostly to friends and gamers." Kerry leaned forward and pointed to a line highlighted in pink. "What's interesting is this call to a Canadian number."

"Another gamer?"

"I don't know. It was made to an untraceable disposable phone."

"Did you ask Colleen about it?"

"Not yet. I found out the phone was sold in Thunder Bay, so I called the Ontario Provincial Police to see if they could trace the buyer, or at least get the security video from the store where it was purchased."

"And?"

"And I'm waiting for a return call."

"You were going to contact the boat owners."

"Shelly's calling them but she's getting frustrated. Over half the time she gets a voicemail and leaves a message. Inevitably, she gets called back when she's actually reached someone. Finding out that most of them weren't anywhere near the marina in the hours before the murder just adds to her frustration."

"That's kind of the nature of an investigation."

Kerry clenched his jaw. "I've explained that to her, but the slow pace of making connections is souring her on the prospect of being something other than a cop driving streets."

I smiled. "I've seen her in Culver's parking lot texting for my entire lunch hour."

Kerry rolled his shoulders like he was getting stiff. "Yeah, she and I have had a discussion about her personal phone use on the job. I don't know if Len was unaware of how she spent her time or if he just chose to ignore the time she was texting and talking on the phone as long as she was in the car."

Kerry's phone chimed as he spoke. He pulled it out and read the text message. "Daryl found something interesting online. Can I use your phone? He doesn't want to share this information over the cellphone.

I stood and Kerry dialed my phone, then punched the speaker function before signaling me to be quiet. I nodded my understanding and locked the door.

"Daryl, what've you got?"

"I'm amazed and disgusted by what people share online."

"Is there something specific you wanted to talk about?"

"Chief, some of these Facebook and Twitter posts are…like reading someone's diary. I mean people post things I wouldn't tell my priest in confession."

"Daryl, focus. What did you find?"

"Well, the Facebook stuff is pretty tame but there's some tweets about sailing stuff. Someone started a conversation with #idiotTHsailors. That started a whole string of tweets with people complaining about the boating skills, or lack thereof, among the people sailing out of Two Harbors."

"Some of the sailors aren't skilled?"

"There's some of that—mostly sailing boat captains complaining about the powerboats; Powerboats failing to give right of way to the sailboats. Powerboats cutting off sailboats. Powerboat wakes flipping kayaks.

"But it's more than that, Chief. There are complaints, but there are people who go way overboard. Here, let me read you one: 'Listen, idiot, if you cut me off again the Coast Guard will find your boat adrift in the lake.' Here's another one: 'Check your gas before you go out again, I wouldn't want you to get out a couple miles and have your motor die because the spark plugs are fouled.'"

Kerry had been staring at me as Daryl read the threats. He shook his head. "I'll call the harbormaster and ask if anyone ever followed through on either of those threats.

Is there anything specific about Art West? Did someone threaten his life?"

"There's nothing overtly threatening. There's a comment about Art bumping someone when he was motoring into the marina, but it just says, 'Hey, idiot. I'll send you the bill for repainting my hull after your oops Saturday.'"

"Find out who sent it and ask them where they were when Art was killed."

"That'll be the easy one. It had an email address attached."

"Is that it, Daryl?"

"Um, have you heard of the Ashley Madison website?"

Kerry looked at me, but I shook my head. "Dolly Madison makes cupcakes, but that's not what you're talking about, right?"

"Cheating spouses put up posts looking for hookups."

"And Art was using that?"

"I didn't find anything from Art, but there's a post from someone calling herself Irish Heat. She's looking for a man to be the *full-service* crew on her sailboat out of Two Harbors. She wants a picture and sailing experience."

"That's interesting, but is it pertinent to the murder?"

Daryl chuckled. "I don't know, but she had some takers and the person who posted it knows how to cover her tracks. Most posts have an IP address that I can use to trace them back to a specific location or computer. Whoever posted this is good. The IP address takes me to a computer, but the IP address attached to this is totally bogus. It doesn't exist. When I try to trace it I get nothing."

"Sounds like whoever is looking for a crew knows her computer stuff."

"Chief, Colleen West is a programmer who'd know how to cover her tracks and she has an Irish name."

"Send her a picture of a cute sailor and create some fake sailing experience? Maybe she'll contact you."

"Irish Heat stopped responding to contacts this week."

Kerry leaned back. "What was going on before?"

"She'd get a contact every day or two and she was responding to them. Lots of them were from the east coast or Florida, but there were a few from Duluth and Superior. She'd flirt with them until she knew where they were located or until she determined they weren't sailors. But the last time she was online was Monday."

I grabbed a piece of paper and wrote one word. Kerry nodded. "Daryl, did Irish Heat ever send a picture of herself to potential sailors?"

"Never. She told a couple of guys she was a cougar who worked out, but she never posted or sent a picture of herself."

"Good work, Daryl. Keep at it and see if you can find anyone who made a specific threat against Art."

"Hang on Chief, Shelly's waving a note at me. I'll have her pick up the line."

"Chief, I actually found someone who was at the marina and heard something that might've been a shot."

"Great! Who is it?"

"Randy Martinson. He said he was working on his head when he heard something. I don't exactly know what he meant about his head, but he went onto the deck and saw two guys carrying a cooler down a pier one over from his."

Kerry looked at me and I mouthed, "a head on a boat is a bathroom."

He nodded his understanding. "Was that about the time of the shooting?"

"I guess so. We don't know exactly when Mr. West was shot. I mean, his body was found Thursday, but that's not when he died, right?"

"Right, the coroner said he'd been dead about forty-eight hours."

"Well, that fits. Randy Martinson saw the two guys right after he ate lunch Tuesday."

"Did he know the two guys?"

"Hang on, let me look at my notes." We heard paper shuffle. "He said one of them was a sportfishing charter captain, named Casey Bradley. He didn't know the other guy but thought he was probably Casey's crew. I guess the crew members turn over pretty often."

"Did you call Casey Bradley?"

"Um, no. I thought you might want to talk with him yourself."

Kerry looked at me and rolled his eyes. "Do you have a number for him?"

"All I could find is the charter service phone number on his webpage." Shelly read the number and Kerry wrote it on a Post-it Note.

"Okay, is there anything else, Shelly?"

"Um, not really. I mean, Randy Martinson said Art West was an amateur, but it wasn't said like he disliked him or anything."

"Have any of the other people offered opinions about the victim?"

"A couple knew him enough to say, hi. But most of the others had heard about the murder but didn't really know Art West."

Kerry shut down the speaker, ending the call. "The harbormaster said Colleen was the sailor and Art was learning. I'm not surprised that people called Art an amateur. I'm sure amateurs irritate some of the more seasoned captains."

Kerry stood, getting ready to leave.

I leaned against the door. "Oh no. You can't tantalize me with all Shelly and Daryl's information and then walk away. Call the harbormaster and Randy Martinson."

Kerry smiled and sat in my desk chair. "What should I ask the harbormaster?"

You told Daryl you'd ask him about the threats of cutting a boat loose or fouling someone's gas. He might even know who calls herself Irish Heat." I pulled up the harbormaster's phone number on my phone and handed it to Kerry.

The call was picked up on the second ring. "Knife River Marina, this is Ray."

"Hi, Ray. This is Chief Stone with a couple questions."

"Huh. The caller I.D. says Whistling Pines."

"I'm at Whistling Pines and a couple questions came up."

"Fire away."

"Randy Martinson might've heard a shot Tuesday when he was working inside his boat. He saw a fishing charter captain and his mate carrying a cooler down the dock when he came topside to check on the noise."

"Okay. What do you want to know?"

"It was early afternoon Tuesday, and he saw Casey Bradley and his mate carrying a cooler down the dock."

"I imagine Casey had a half-day charter and they were carrying in their client's catch."

"Can you check your records and see if…"

"Hang on, Chief. I don't book the charters. If someone calls looking for a fishing charter, I'll give them the name of a captain, but they do their own bookings. I just rotate through the list and give out numbers."

"Did you give Casey's name to anyone for a Tuesday charter?"

"Like I said, I don't keep records, per se. I don't recall giving Casey's name to anyone, but like I told you, my memory isn't what it used to be."

"Do you know if Casey had any complaints about Art West?"

"I've never heard anything. Their slips are on different docks, so if Casey had a complaint about Art I'd guess it was because of something outside the marina."

"I want to run something else past you." Kerry related the twitter complaints and asked if they matched any actual acts of vandalism.

"I haven't heard about those, specifically. You know, a couple people a year get water in their gas or forget to change their spark plugs and their engines die on the lake. I don't think those are sabotage, but it's hard to say one way or the other. No one's complained or accused anyone else of fouling their gas, and I've never had a boat drift away unless their boat wasn't tied up properly…or someone was too drunk to deal with their lines."

"Someone wanted Art West to pay for repainting his boat."

Ray chuckled. "Yeah, that was a knot problem. Ray left his lines too long and his boat rubbed against the hull of the sailboat in the other half of his slip for almost a week. Art apologized and paid the other captain for half a repainting job."

I leaned close. "Do you know any boat captains who call themselves Irish Heat?"

"I don't know anyone who goes by that nickname but, there's a sailboat named Irish Heat."

Kerry's eyes lit up. "Is it Ray and Colleen West's boat?"

"It belongs to Pat Flannagan. Why are you asking?"

Kerry took a deep breath and blew it out. "Does Pat's wife ever take the boat out with a male crew other than her husband?"

There was a long pause. "Chief, remember when I told you that I sometimes don't see everything that happens around the harbor?"

"Ray, this is serious."

Ray sighed. "It's none of my business who Jen Flanagan has as her crew. That's as plain as I can put it."

Kerry looked at me and I shrugged. "Have you thought of anyone else who might've had a beef with Art West?"

123

"He was an amateur sailor, but he was no worse than a lot of people who moor their boats here. So, from a sailing standpoint..."

Kerry looked at me like I should know why Ray stopped speaking. "Ray, are you still there?"

"Hang on for a second, Chief."

Kerry muted the phone. "This is strange. I wonder what's going on?"

"Maybe someone came in to pay their fees."

Ray was back a minute later. "Are you still there, Chief?"

Kerry unmuted the phone. "Yes. Is everything okay?"

"Yeah, I just sold a couple kids some soda pop and shooed them out." Ray paused. "There's something going on among the sailboat racers. A few captains are serious, and a lot of the others view it as a social outing. Colleen West is a serious sailboat captain, and she races hard. Art's an amateur and he makes rookie mistakes."

"So, Colleen gets after him?"

"Not really. I mean Art beats himself up some, but a couple of the other serious captains have been mad at Art when he messes up on the boat."

"Give me an example."

"Colleen was coming about during a race, and Art had the boom belayed on the windward side. She turned, but the boom didn't swing, so their sail went slack. They were in the lead and the boats behind them had to veer off port and starboard to keep from ramming them. There were two captains who lodged formal complaints with the Duluth Yacht Club and asked the board to sanction Wests from competition."

"That hardly sounds like a murder motive."

Ray laughed. "There are a lot of things that aren't murder motives when you're sober. After a few rounds at the bar and encouragement from the other captains... Well, you know how fish stories go. Well, sailing is no different. Small infractions get to be gross threats to life and equipment by the time the bar closes."

Kerry looked at me and shrugged. "Who were the other captains?"

"Chief, I heard about the incident second hand. You'd best talk to the yacht club and see who lodged the complaints."

Kerry hung up and continued to stare at the phone. "Love, drugs, and money are the three most likely murder motives. Getting cut off in a sailboat regatta hardly makes the list."

"Like Ray said, lots of things look different through the bottom of a whiskey glass."

Picking up the Post-it Note, Kerry dialed Casey Bradley's number and put it on speaker. It rang three times and rolled over to voicemail. "Hi Casey, this is Chief Stone.

I'm investigating Art West's murder and I'd like to ask if you heard a gunshot in the marina on Tuesday. Please call my cellphone." Kerry ended the message by leaving his number. He looked at me. "Look up the number for the Duluth Yacht Club. I'm going to ask them who lodged complaints against Art and Colleen over the sailing incident."

"I hate to be a killjoy, Kerry but I have to work."

Kerry got up and stood facing me. "Len said he tried to get you to work for him because you were the best investigator he had. Has your opinion changed?"

"No, Kerry, I don't want to be a cop. Not now. Not ever." I put out my hand. "But I would like to consider you a friend. My door is always open."

Kerry shook my hand and smiled. "The leads I've got are thin and not promising. I could use another investigator pressing ahead on this. The city council told me to hire a replacement now that Len's gone."

I leaned forward. "It's early in the investigation. Something will turn up."

Kerry ran his fingers through his hair. "Peter, this is my first murder investigation as chief. People expect it to be solved."

I opened the door. "It will be."

"I wish I was as confident as you are. I've never solved a crime with this little evidence."

Kerry left and I stared at the door, reflecting on my conversations with Len, the now retired chief. *How did I become the police chief's confidant?*

Putting that thought aside, I printed out guitar chords for three sea shanties. I tuned my guitar and strummed the chords, humming the melodies and losing myself in the music.

I closed my eyes and my thoughts drifted to the days after my father's death. My mother was devastated and found solace with our neighbors and her friends. I was lost, without a support network. I'd spent days in my room, strumming the same guitar. It was then I'd become a musician, the person who became one with his instrument. I'd learned chords and songs. The theory of songs and chord progression became second nature to me. I'd learned to play every contemporary song and could pick up my guitar and master any new song in minutes.

From there my thoughts drifted to Iraq, where I'd played in the barracks with Marines gathered around me. It was an escape for all of us, a piece of normal in a world of insanity. I pictured the faces, the men who'd come home intact, the one's I'd treated who eventually lost limbs, and the ones who'd returned in caskets. I moved on to playing to vets in the VFW and then to Whistling Pines, Jenny, and Jeremy.

With eyes closed, I had vision of the future, a baby in Jenny's arms, me at her side. I started picking *Brahm's Lullaby*. Tears filled my eyes.

"Peter?"

My eyes popped open and I wiped my cheeks on my sleeve. "Yeah."

Howard Johnson walked in and closed the door. Howard was a Korean war vet who never spoke about his military experience. A shadow box in his apartment contained captain's bars, a purple heart, a bronze star, and service ribbons. That was everything I knew about his time in the Army.

"Are you okay?' he asked softly.

Setting the guitar back in the corner I said, "Yes. I just took a trip down memory lane."

"There are some historical lanes I resist traveling."

I nodded. "Smiling faces of men who didn't come home."

Howard didn't say anything, but I knew the faces he pictured weren't smiling, but bloody and shattered. There was no need for either of us to mention those.

"What's up?" I asked.

"This is a bit of a jump from nostalgia, but I wanted to run a thought past you. Do you think we could serve a bit of rum during the singalong?"

"Rum? Really?"

"I think it'd be a fun addition to the pirate theme."

"Howard, half our residents stagger around when they're sober."

"The British Navy used to issue drams of grog to the sailors. It was half and half, rum and water. If we made grog and garnished it with a wedge of lime…"

I stood up. "Let's see if Nancy's in her office."

We found Nancy leafing through a magazine. "I think I'm about to be blindsided by a crazy idea," she said, setting her reading aside.

"Howard suggested serving grog, watered down rum, during our singalong. I think the residents would get a kick out of it."

Nancy smiled. "That's inspired, Howard. Yes! We can put up some announcements and we'll have the best turnout of the year. Let's do it!"

I hesitated. "Who'll buy the rum?"

Nancy opened a desk drawer and pulled out a wallet. "I have discretionary petty cash; if one of you would go to the liquor store, I'll pay."

Howard stood. "I've got nothing else going on. I'll buy a couple bottles of Captain Morgan and a bag of limes."

"Perfect!" Nancy said, handing Howard sixty dollars. "I'll ask the kitchen to find plastic glasses."

I hesitated. "Small glasses, like four ounces."

Nancy laughed. "Agreed."

* * *

Jeremy washed the supper dishes while I dried. Jenny was watching a sappy movie on a cable channel. I'd caught just enough of it to recognize the main characters—a pauper and a rich debutante—to recognize them as the handmaiden and prince from the previous night's movie. The plot would be the same; the pauper would be revealed as a duke or prince and would carry away the young woman to live happily forever after.

Jeremy drained the dishwater and stepped down from the stool that got him high enough to reach the sink. "What are we doing tonight?" he asked.

"Are you through with your homework?"

"Dad…"

"Let me check your math."

Jeremy slogged into the dining room and pulled a worksheet out of his backpack. We sat together, going through his math, and making a couple corrections. He was resigned to my assistance but would've been happy to turn in the homework with the mistakes.

"Now what?"

I pushed my chair away from the table. "Dolores said there's a pirate costume in a trunk downstairs."

"That's lit!"

I didn't understand the meaning of *lit*, but assumed it meant something good or interesting. I switched on the basement lights and we descended the creaking wooden steps. Three old incandescent bulbs cast a dim yellow light in the middle of the basement, leaving the corners nearly dark. I made a mental note to buy some LED bulbs to brighten up the space.

"What kind of box is the costume in?"

"She said it was in a trunk."

Jeremy stopped and looked at me. "A trunk, like the back of a car?"

"A steamer trunk. It's a big box with a hinged lid. People used them when they took steamship trips across the ocean. They'd pack all their clothes in them."

"Didn't they have suitcases?"

"The trunks are more durable and kept their things from getting crushed when they were loaded under lots of other things inside the stowage area of the ship."

Jeremy pointed to an area along the wall under the living room. "There are some big things in the corner with a rug on top."

I carefully folded the dusty rug and set it aside, exposing a pair of steamer trunks and some cardboard boxes. The hinge creaked ominously as I opened the first trunk. Jeremy started pulling clothing out and piling it on the floor until I intervened and made sure everything had been as neatly folded as it was inside the trunk.

"These are dresses," he said, holding up an evening gown that appeared to have been from the 1930s. It was from a time when Dolores was probably the belle of the ball, with sequins and fringe. I'd always known Dolores as an older woman who wore support hose and orthopedic shoes. Under the dress were a pair of high-heeled shoes and a box with genuine silk stockings.

I took the dress from him gently and held it up. "I bet this was something Dolores wore to a fancy party."

Jeremy pulled out a corset with snaps to attach the silk stockings. "What's this?"

"It's a piece of lady's underwear."

Jeremy dropped it like it could've caused the plague. "Yuk."

I stacked the dresses back in the trunk. "Let's look in the other trunk."

It's hinges were badly rusted and gave way only after I pulled hard on the lid. They shrieked in displeasure as I lifted the top and leaned it against the wall.

Jeremy grabbed an oblong box off the top and removed the lid. "It's a weird hat with a feather."

I lifted out what I thought of as an admiral's bicorn hat with an ostrich plume extending from the back.

"Why is it long and flat? I thought pirates wore hats that have three corners."

"It's called a bicorn hat, because it has two corners, front and back. Only high-ranking officers wore bicorn hats, and they only wore them for special occasions requiring their fanciest uniforms." I put it on. "What do you think?"

"It makes you look like a loser."

Under the box was a double-breasted black coat with brass buttons, and matching pants with satin stripes down the seams. Jeremy pulled out a white shirt. "There aren't any buttons."

"In the old days, fancy shirts didn't have buttons. They put little metal things, called studs, in the matching buttonholes. There's probably a little box in here with studs and cufflinks for the shirt."

Jeremy dug around the edges, looking for the box of studs while I pulled out a wide belt with a loop intended for a scabbard. Jeremy emerged with a box. The lid stuck, and when he pulled it loose, the studs and cufflinks exploded, spreading the contents over the dirty basement floor.

"Oops."

"Pick them up."

He sighed, then noticed the belt I was holding. "Why does the belt have a loop?"

"That's where the sword scabbard was attached."

His eyes lit up. "There's a sword?"

"You pick up the studs, and I'll look for the sword."

The trunk was obviously too small to accommodate a sword. Tucked behind it I spotted an oily rag set on a pair of bricks to keep it off the sometimes-moist basement floor. Jeremy abandoned the hunt for the studs to watch me unwrap the rags. Inside, was a brass scabbard with a sword. The sword's handle appeared to be real ivory and the butt was fashioned as a knight's helmet. A small chain ran from the butt to the hilt on one side. I held the sword with the rag, afraid it would tarnish if my fingers touched it.

Jeremy sensed my reverence and looked at it in awe. "Is it real?"

"I think so."

"Let's show Mom."

"Pick up the rest of the studs and we'll take the whole uniform upstairs."

Something about Dolores' earlier conversation nagged at me just beyond the realm of consciousness. I held my hand on the trunk lid, thinking. I finally bent down and dug through the other treasures in the trunk. I found several Masonic items, a Shriner's fez and sashes, then my fingers hit something solid. Pushing clothing aside, I pulled out a small bulky item wrapped in dark waxed paper.

With the studs in his hand, Jeremy stood at my shoulder. "What's that?"

I unwrapped the paper, exposing a muzzle-loading pistol. Jeremy reached for the pistol and I held it away from him. "This isn't a toy."

"Dad, I just wanted to see it."

Thinking of Dolores' admonition, I said, "Look with your eyes, not your hands." I removed the ramrod and slid it into the barrel until it stopped three quarters of the way to the breech. It was loaded.

"What are you doing?"

Pulling back the hammer, I made sure there wasn't a cap on the firing nipple and let out a breath. I eased the hammer back. "Checking to see if it's loaded."

"Is it?"

"Um, yes and no. There's no firing cap, but it feels like there's a powder charge in the barrel."

"Let's shoot it!"

I wrapped the gun in the rags and paper. "I don't have a firing cap and I'm not sure it's safe."

"What are you going to do with it?"

"I'm going to ask someone how to unload it."

Jenny held a box of tissues on her lap and damp tissues were scattered around her on the couch as credits from the sappy holiday movie rolled on the screen. She looked up, her eyes red from crying, as I carried the oily rag and uniform into the living room. Jeremy followed with the hatbox and studs.

"We found my pirate costume." I set the sword and pistol on the coffee table and unfolded the coat and pants.

"Fancy," she said. "Does it fit?"

I pulled on the coat. The sleeves were a tad short and the jacket itself was loose. "I think Dolores' husband was a bit shorter and heavier than me, but it'll do."

Jeremy pulled open the hatbox. "Tell Dad this makes him look like a loser." He held the hat out to me, and I put it on.

Jenny laughed out loud. "You look like Admiral Farragut. 'Darn the torpedoes, full speed ahead!'"

I glanced between them, knowing she'd paraphrased the Farragut quote, and hoping Jeremy didn't recognize it.

"What are the things wrapped in rags?"

"It's a real sword and gun, Mom."

Jeremy reached for the sword, but I swept it out of his hands. "It appears to be a Masonic ceremonial sword." I gently unwrapped the item and held it for her to see. "The handle might be real ivory with scrimshaw."

Jenny put her hand over her mouth. "I suppose it's valuable."

"I'll have to do some research, but you're probably right. It's illegal to import or own ivory but I think antiquities are exempt under the law." I set the sword on the coffee table

136

and unwrapped the pistol. "This was in the bottom of the steamer trunk." I held the muzzle-loading pistol carefully by the wooden handle, not touching the barrel or ornamental brass.

Jenny glanced at Jeremy. "Dolores left us another legacy that shoots."

"Dad says it's loaded."

Jenny's eyes darted to me. "You didn't unload it?"

"It's complicated. There's no cartridge to remove. The powder charge is poured in the muzzle, then a lead bullet is pressed in."

"Can't you pour them out?"

I shook my head while rewrapping the gun. "It doesn't pour out. It's packed tight so the bullet and powder don't fall out when it's carried."

"Ah, like when it's jammed under a pirate's belt."

"Exactly," I said picking up the clothing, pistol, and sword.

"Are you planning to wear this to the costume competition?"

"I'm not competing, but yes, I thought I'd wear it tomorrow for the singalong."

"What about the pistol?"

"I'll put that away until I can find someone who knows how to unload it."

Nodding her approval, Jenny said, "I'm sure Dolores will be pleased."

"I think the uniform will get lots of laughs."

Chapter Seven

The phone rang shortly after I'd tucked in Jeremy for the night. "Hello."

"I spoke with Casey Bradley and he claims they were out on a full-day charter Tuesday, so didn't hear a shot and couldn't have been the person who was seen on the dock."

I stepped onto the back step and closed the door. A swarm of gnats were drawn to the glowing cellphone screen. "Our cook's husband is a charter captain and he saw Casey going back to the marina before noon, Tuesday."

"I called Randy Martinson and reconfirmed that with him. He's certain it was Casey and his mate on the dock Tuesday afternoon. He remembers seeing Casey's boat, and seeing Casey and his mate carrying a big cooler. He said the cooler was green with a white lid and was probably at least ninety-six quarts. It looked like it was loaded with something because the two guys were struggling under the weight."

"But Casey claimed he was out of the marina."

"That's Casey's story. I didn't say I was buying it."

"What are you going to do now?"

Kerry paused. "I've got to determine why Casey doesn't want to admit being on the dock Tuesday."

"He might not want to get involved. You know, the fishing season is short and if he gets dragged in for depositions and testimony in a trial, he could lose a big percentage of his annual income."

"I've got his mate's name. Lance Peters has been arrested a couple times for drunken driving and is on probation. He's not in any position to lie about his whereabouts."

"Sounds like you've got some real investigating to do and some solid suspects."

"I also need to follow up with Jen Flannagan about her sudden departure from the cheating website. I wonder if Art was one of the crewmembers she'd recruited?"

"I hadn't considered that. I suppose there may have been a messy breakup, or someone's spouse found out about it."

"She hasn't returned my messages, so I'll have to confront her in person."

After hiding the pistol in the deepest recesses of our closet shelving, I tried on the entire Masonic outfit later that evening. The pant's waist was too large, but a belt rectified that. The legs were an inch too short, but I decided against trying to alter them. They'd been cuffed for eighty or more years and the wool fabric would resist any attempt to remove the crease, if it would even come out. I opted instead for white socks and black shoes, hoping the pants would look somewhat like knickers instead of pants in need of alteration.

I'd hardly set my costume down in my office when the phone rang.

"Peter, I've got a problem."

I recognized Meg Cochran's voice. "What's the problem?"

"You suggested I contact the Sons of Norway. I met with them last night to enlist their participation in the festival and, well, I've lost control. I think a couple of the Swedes were tipping some aquavit before the meeting. An argument broke out."

"They don't want to participate?"

Meg laughed. "Oh no, they want to take it over."

"What do you mean by 'argument and take it over?'"

"They voted to move their annual picnic to this weekend. Then they started throwing out ideas, and people volunteered to do things."

"That all sounds good."

"Believe me, I struggle to motivate people to volunteer for anything, but this was out of control. They're going to convert Matt Larson's sailboat into a Viking longboat. Four guys are probably at the lumberyard as we speak, buying plywood and paint to make the transformation. Two women are calling all the regional lutefisk companies."

I thought back to Brian's comments about the lutefisk throwing contest and groaned. "They're trying to find lutefisk for the throwing contest."

"That too, but they're going to host a lutefisk lunch in the park! They're planning to serve baked lutefisk with white sauce, mashed rutabagas and potatoes, and boiled potato sausage."

"That sounds…interesting. Is that what caused the argument?"

"Yes! I can't believe it. They got into it over whether they should bake or boil the lutefisk. There's a whole bunch of them who think it's got to be boiled to be authentic. Then, there's another bunch who argued that boiling it would stink up the whole town and cause 'runny' lutefisk. I guess the baked version has more body and is less slimy."

"Oh."

"Oh, hardly covers it."

"What did they decide?"

"The bakers out-voted the boilers, thank heavens. The thought of hundreds of tourists coming to a town stinking of boiling lutefisk had me ready to resign."

"It settled down in the end?"

"I think cooler heads will prevail after they all sober up, but the wheels are turning and I'm not entirely sure what's going to happen."

"Just let them run with it. I'm sure the tourists will be amused even if the lutefisk feed isn't a big draw."

"Hang on, Peter. I'm adding the Sons of Norway activities to the website." I heard keys clicking. "Um, is lutefisk capitalized?"

"I don't think so but let me check the internet." I typed in lutefisk capitalization, then laughed. "The Portland State University guide to capitalization popped up."

"No way. The Portlandians considered the capitalization of lutefisk something worthy of mention?"

"It's incidental to another issue. Listen to this, from the Portland State University style manual. 'The president will represent PSU at the funeral of Henning Morthall, the Svensson professor of Scandinavian literature at Yale, who died last week from an overdose of lutefisk.' The word lutefisk is not capitalized."

"You're kidding, someone used that line in a publication?"

"Some clever person thought that was a good way to illustrate how to handle the capitalization of college titles and departments. They also dealt with the capitalization of lutefisk."

"Who's going to clean up the lutefisk after they toss it in the street? I mean, it stinks and is slippery. I have visions of people slipping and falling, then suing the city."

I laughed out loud.

"This is NOT funny."

"Have the fire department park a tanker up the hill from the competition. They can hose down the street and wash the lutefisk into the storm sewers."

"Oh, good plan." Meg paused. "No, wait. Do we need a permit from the Minnesota Pollution Control Agency to wash lutefisk into storm sewers that feed into Lake Superior? Will we get fined?"

"Who's going to tell the PCA?"

Meg sighed. "I heard Len Rentz and his wife are going to Canada for the weekend. I may join them."

"Did you talk to the Rotary club?"

"Yes, they're serving a pancake breakfast Saturday morning. The Jaycees are going to make signs and direct people to parking. John Carr talked to the bandshell fundraising committee and they're going to use the concert as a fundraiser, passing the hat during the music. The historical society is going to have extra staff in the depot to handle the surge in visitors and there will be lighthouse tours. I think we'll have plenty of activities to keep the tourists satisfied."

"How about the sailboat regatta?"

"The yacht club is on board. The president is sure they'll have at least a dozen captains participating. He's a little nervous about the Sons of Norway ship, but they'll deal with it."

"A couple of my residents have been searching for the medallion. There were rumors it was found in a jar of pickled herring bought at the grocery store."

"What? In pickled herring?"

"It was one of the stupid rumors that circulates here. If there isn't a good rumor, someone starts one."

"As far as I know, the medallion hasn't been recovered yet."

"I assume more clues will be coming."

"The radio station broadcasts new clues at 6 a.m. and 3 p.m."

"Is the hunt generating a lot of interest?"

"It's been a hit with the local residents. I imagine it'll be a zoo on Saturday when the tourists really start filling the motels. If the medallion isn't found before then, of course."

"I assume the last clue will be specific?"

Meg chuckled. "Unless a pack rat hauled the medallion away, I think a dozen people will converge on the hiding spot at three Saturday afternoon." Meg paused. "How are the Whistling Pines festivities going?"

"There's confusion about this being a naturist cruise, versus a naturalist cruise. Someone keeps posting signup sheets for a naturalist cruise. I have dozens of people ready to go. Half think it's a birdwatching event and the rest want to see naked bodies. They're going to be very disappointed when it doesn't happen."

Meg's pause was too long. "I got a call from a tour boat operator out of Superior. His boat can accommodate forty-six people at a time, and he's willing to take out morning and afternoon cruises."

"That's a problem?"

"The North Shore Naturists have reserved half the seats for the morning sailing."

"You're kidding? Nudists have reserved half the seats?"

"Yes. They've got twenty people signed up so far, which leaves room for twenty-six other passengers."

I groaned.

"You know Wendy, right?"

"She's the Whistling Pines assistant director and the lead singer of the Gin Fizzes."

"Wendy called, the tour operator and reserved sixteen seats on the morning naturist sailing."

I let out a breath. "The Whistling Pines van seats sixteen people."

"I think that's not a coincidence."

I thought of Jenny's comments about stocking up on aloe for sunburned residents after the cruise. "I've got to talk to the director."

"Peter."

"What?"

"I'd rather see your residents filling seats than have a captain lose money when he's trying to help us by providing tourist activities."

"But…"

"Take off your protective hat and think about the tourism money this is bringing to town."

"I don't see nudists and wrinkled retirees as a good mix."

"I heard most of the naturists are older adults. It might not be a bad mix."

"I have one resident who wants to see six-pack abs."

"I'd advise you to lower her expectations."

I sighed. "Is that everything?"

Meg laughed. "The two Lutheran Churches are in competition."

"For what? To see who can save the most heathen Vikings?"

"They're right across the parking lot from each other and they decided since the Sons of Norway and a food truck were serving lunch, they're going to serve dinner after the band concert."

I grimaced. "Please tell me they're not doing more lutefisk."

"The Norwegian Lutheran Church is serving chicken and mashed potatoes. The Swedish Lutheran Church decided to outdo them by serving Swedish meatballs, lefse, and Jell-O salads."

"Those sound just like the menus the Lutheran women prepare for funerals. They specialize in Jell-O salads with fruit. I've had everything from canned pears to mandarin oranges in gelatin at funerals I've attended."

"It'd be best if you kept that information to yourself."

"Are the restaurant owners okay with all these extra meals being served?"

"Ha! They are concerned about being able to handle the hundreds of extra tourists who are going to be in town. They're relieved and figure there will be enough people not interested in standing in line and eating on picnic tables that they'll be swamped anyway."

"How about the other businesses?"

"Everyone's happy. The hotels are booked. The campground is full. The grocery store is ordering extra stock. I've never seen so many people in my antiques shop, and it's not even the weekend yet."

"It sounds like a boon to business."

Meg's pause worried me. "I'm not sure anyone's excited about the liquor store's plans for a free rum tasting. Marvin's planning to have a 'comely wench' pouring samples and Chief Stone has already requested they limit the number of samples per person and his wench's costume be not too comely."

"Who's going to be the wench and how comely are we talking?"

"Karen Krueger is pouring the samples, and Marv was elusive when I asked about what he meant by comely."

I pictured Karen, the divorced assistant manager. She had personality and spark, along with an attractive, forty-something full figure. She always unbuttoned her shirt too far and wore skin-tight jeans. Karen was personally responsible for keeping a lot of male customers from driving to Duluth for lower liquor prices at the chain stores.

"Do you need anything else from me?" I asked.

"Buccaneer Days is now barrelling ahead under its own momentum. I don't think anyone can change its speed or trajectory."

I ended the conversation with Meg and went to the director's office. Nancy was walking out the door as I approached, so I hailed her. "We need to talk."

"About?"

"There is going to be a naturist cruise and Wendy reserved sixteen seats for our residents."

"Naturist not naturalist?" Nancy asked.

"Nudists not birdwatchers."

Nancy tried to hide her grin. "Let's see if Wendy's in the dining room."

Wendy and Dolores, my former neighbor, were in the back of the room huddling over a catalog. Dolores turned the publication so we could see what they were looking at. "Wendy thinks she can get a costume here overnight. I think I'll make a fine wench in this, don't you?"

The costume was very conservative. High-necked blouse with long sleeves and ruffled cuffs. The skirt was long and meant to look like it was tattered.

I pulled out a chair for Nancy and sat across from Dolores. "I think that'll be fine."

Dolores nodded to Wendy, who was apparently ready to place the order on her smartphone. She punched a button and set the phone on the table next to her partially completed crossword puzzle.

Nancy smiled and folded her hands. "Peter just got word a Superior cruise operator is bringing his boat over for the Buccaneer Days festival."

Wendy nodded. "I know. I was the one who asked him to contact the chamber of commerce with the idea after the North Shore Nudist Club struck out with their usual boat captain."

Nancy glanced at me and chuckled. "I should've known."

"He's doing the naturist trip in the morning and a family trip in the afternoon. The chamber guaranteed he'd sell at least half the seats, so Meg was pleased that Whistling Pines was bringing sixteen people for the morning sailing."

Nancy weighed her words carefully. "It appears you've got the people to fill the van.

Do they all realize it's going to involve nudity?"

Dolores jumped in before Wendy could reply. "Why, yes! I'm sure people are looking forward to it. Hulda Packer bought a bikini for the trip."

Nancy looked at Dolores with shock. "Hulda owns a bikini?"

"Wendy helped her order it."

Nancy clenched her eyes shut, trying to erase an image from her mind. "Wendy?"

"Hulda wanted a bikini and I helped her find one."

Nancy drew a breath and let it out slowly. "As long as everyone involved understands what they're getting into and we don't have anyone who expects birdwatching. It won't be warm. Please make sure they bring coats or blankets."

Wendy put up her hands. "I've been very clear. This involves nudity and they know it might be cool on the water."

Nancy leaned on her elbows and whispered. "I want to be clear. It will NOT involve any of my staff in the buff."

That caught Wendy off guard. "I suppose I'll have to wear a beach coverup."

Nancy got up. "You do what you think is appropriate, but I don't want to hear about any previously unviewed tattoos. Understood?"

"But what if I have a wardrobe malfunction?"

"Make sure, 'what if' doesn't happen."

Nancy walked out with the three of us watching. "Killjoy," Wendy uttered when Nancy was out of earshot.

Dolores lost interest and turned to me. "Did you find the pirate costme?"

"Jeremy and I found the trunk last night. I tightened the belt a bit to keep the pants up, but it'll be a hit."

"How was the sword? It didn't rust, did it?"

"It was nicely wrapped in oilcloth and was in perfect condition. I was surprised by the handle. Is it real ivory?"

Dolores nodded. "And the hilt is sterling silver."

"Jeremy wasn't impressed with the bicorn hat. Jenny said it reminded her of Admiral Farragut navigating Mobile Bay."

Dolores smiled. "Farragut was America's first and possibly most noted Naval hero. He climbed the rigging of his flagship, the Hartford, so he could see the battle. When his lead ship hit a mine the column started to slow, bringing them under fire from the Rebel shore guns. 'Damn the torpedoes! Full speed ahead, Drayton! Hard a starboard! Ring four bells! Eight bells! Sixteen bells!'"

Wendy frowned. "I thought Navy bells marked time."

I shook my head. "In old steamships, the helm communicated with the boiler room with bells. Four bells meant full steam. Farragut was asking for full steam, and more."

"Did he live through the battle?" Wendy asked.

"He lived through the battle and sunk or captured the entire Rebel fleet in Mobile Bay. The Army came in from behind the city and cut off one of the major seaports the Confederacy was using to be resupplied by foreign allies."

Wendy waved her hands. "I'm on history overload. Tell me about your costume."

"It has a bicorn hat with an ostrich plume. The coat is double-breasted with tails."

Wendy nodded. "And there's a real sword."

Dolores shook her head. "It's a Masonic ceremonial sword, not a military sword."

Wendy looked deflated. "So, a fake sword."

"It's a real steel sword, just very ornate," I replied.

That perked her up. "When do I get to see this outfit?"

I looked at the clock. "At two o'clock when we lead the singalong."

Wendy looked shocked. "Crap! I forgot my wench costume. I'll have to go home over lunch."

I smiled at Dolores. "Do you think anyone would miss her if she left for home now?"

Dolores raised her eyebrows without answering and got up.

Wendy gathered her crossword, pencil, and phone. She stopped for one second with her armload of stuff. "Remember, sailor, I get even if you pull a prank on me."

I was walking to my office when Margaret waved to me in the commons. She motioned for me to join her behind the aviary. "Have you arrested Artie's wife yet?"

"I'm the recreation director, not a cop. And I don't know that she's even a suspect in Art's murder. She was very emotional when the police chief told her he'd been killed."

"She's been in trouble before. She was arrested back east for something before she married Artie."

"She seems like a normal, well adjusted person. I don't see her as a murderer."

Margaret frowned at me. "You check her criminal record back east. She lived in…one of those states that starts with 'New.'"

"New Jersey or New York?"

Margaret shook her head. "Those aren't it. Maybe it starts with 'North.'"

She turned and walked away. "I knew that none of the New England states started with North. Margaret was confused and maybe a little vindictive, and I wasn't going to get sucked into her delusions about Colleen West.

I drove into town and bought a sub sandwich, Wendy's admonition about getting even ringing in my ears. Her retribution took many forms over the years, from leaving inappropriate images scrolling on my office computer screen to embarrassing me in front of a crowd at Hugo's bar when I was playing with her band. The payback sometimes came immediately, but other times simmered for weeks before boiling over on me.

I was wrapped up in my thoughts when Kerry surprised me by slipping into the booth. "Lance Peters doesn't have a phone listing, so I called his probation officer. Lance is employed by Casey and has been reporting in as required. I got his cellphone number and left a voicemail."

"Did Lance's probation officer have anything else to say about Lance?"

"He's living with his girlfriend in an upstairs duplex. He's been attending AA meetings, calling in regularly, reporting for and passing random drug and alcohol tests, and by all accounts is being a law-abiding citizen."

"But..."

"There were no buts. His PO said Lance seems to have his shit together." Kerry glanced over his shoulder. "I'll get a sub and join you if you're going to stay for a couple minutes."

There were two texts from Jenny about upcoming commitments with her parents and a voicemail from a telemarketer that I deleted. I was texting Jenny when Kerry sat down.

"Is Jeremy in Cub Scouts?"

"Jenny's never had the time to do much more than work and make sure Jeremy does his homework. So no, he's never been to a meeting."

Kerry unwrapped his sub and took a bite. "Jacob's scouting friend is moving and he's going to ask Jeremy to join his cub pack. I hope that's okay."

"It's okay with me. I assume Jeremy will be interested. He thinks Jacob walks on water."

"Deb would like to invite Jeremy to spend a couple nights at our house after the baby is born, to give you and Jenny a day or two to get settled. If you're amenable, she'll sell it as a sleepover. I'm sure the boys will be excited about it."

"That's really nice. I'll tell Jenny." I paused as Kerry fumbled while adjusting the sandwich wrapper. It made me aware of the limited dexterity his scarred left fingers had. "Did anyone on the city council express concern about your burned hand?"

Kerry shook his head while he chewed and swallowed. "I think they were too politically correct to mention my scars."

"Are they a problem?"

Kerry drank from his straw, then paused. "You're the only person other than my doctor who's ever asked that question."

"Knowing what you, and others went through makes me uniquely qualified to ask."

Kerry shook his head and took another bite. "No, being my friend makes you uniquely qualified to ask."

I folded my sandwich wrapper and stuffed it into my drink cup. "You didn't answer the question."

"It depends on what I'm trying to do. Most things only take one hand, and many others only require a second hand to hold things." Kerry paused. "Would I rather have the full use of both hands? Yes. Can I function the way I am? Yes."

"If you need some help around the house, I'm only a phone call away."

"I appreciate that. We hire people to do most household repairs and lawn maintenance. If I get in a bind, I'll give you a call."

Kerry's phone buzzed and he wiped his hand before pulling it from his pocket. "Stone."

I slid my tray to the edge of the table, preparing to leave and give Kerry privacy.

He put up a finger and I slid back into the booth.

"Hi, Lance. Thanks for returning my call."

Half conversation yielded the news that Lance was working for Casey Bradley and had been since May. Kerry asked some general questions, then got to the point of the call. "Were you and Casey in the marina Tuesday?"

Kerry looked to see if anyone was listening, then held the phone out so I could hear Lance's answer. "Um, chief. I think you already talked to Casey about Tuesday."

"Were you in the marina?"

Lance's voice got very soft and Kerry had to hold the phone to his ear to hear the answer.

"Lance, quit beating around the bush. Two people saw you there, and your probation officer said you were a good guy who was going to cooperate. If I need to, I'll pick you up and we can have this discussion in the police station."

Kerry held the phone out so I could hear. Lance let out a sigh. "I need this job, Chief Stone."

"I'm not trying to get you fired, but Art West was shot and killed Tuesday. I need to know what you heard."

"I heard something that sounded like a motor backfiring. I couldn't tell where the sound came from."

"What time was that?"

"About noon. No, closer to one o'clock. I'd hosed down the deck and eaten my sandwich."

"Did you see anyone around West's boat?"

"I guess I'm not sure which one is theirs. A guy's head popped up from the cabin of a sailboat right after the sound. He looked around like he'd heard the sound too and was trying to see where it came from."

"Did you recognize him?"

"Sure. It was Slick, my insurance guy. He was on his boat with…"

"We know about Slick's lunch hour visitors. Was he on his own boat?"

"Yeah, his slip isn't far from us so we see him all the time. He was on his own boat."

"Did you see anyone else?"

"Nope. It was as quiet as it is most weekdays in the afternoon."

"Was Casey with you?"

"Um, yeah."

"He didn't shoot the gun."

"No. We were carrying a cooler, so he was right with me."

"Thanks, Lance."

"That's it?"

"Yes, unless you've got something more to add."

"No."

I put up my finger and whispered. "How many cars were in the parking lot?"

Kerry asked the question.

159

"I don't remember exactly. There were a few, but it wasn't busy like it is on the weekend. It can be a zoo this time of year."

"Were there any cars that seemed out of place or were unusual?"

"Tuesday? I'm sorry, I can't remember what cars I see which day. We're down there every day and the cars and trucks change."

"Thanks, Lance. Call me if you think of anything."

"Um, Chief. Can we keep this between us? I don't want to make Casey mad."

"Casey will never know we had this conversation."

Kerry ended the call and put the phone away. "Do you think Lance was being honest?"

"He sounded sincere and told you things he didn't want shared with his boss. Unless he was the killer, I think he was truthful."

"What motive would he have?"

I got up with my tray. "We don't know what motive anyone had."

Kerry wiped his mouth and threw the paper napkin on his tray. Standing up and seeing no one close he whispered, "Thanks for the words of encouragement, smartass."

I smiled. "Isn't that what friends are for?"

Putting his hand on my shoulder, he guided me to the door.

* * *

I changed into my pirate costume, picked up my guitar, and walked to the community room where we scheduled larger gatherings. Several residents smiled, winked, waved, and said "Arr, a pirate," as I passed.

Bingle, the maintenance man, was setting up the last row of chairs. He looked up from his work and stared at me, his mouth agape. "Are you Blackbeard?"

"No beard, so I must be Jack Sparrow."

Bingle nodded. "You're too clean cut to be a pirate. You need to smear some ash on your face and maybe darken your eyes."

"I am what I am."

"That's Popeye. He's not a pirate." He studied my outfit for a second. "You're a sailor, right?"

"I was in the Navy."

A smile spread over his face as residents started filing in. "It looks like you just got promoted to admiral."

He turned and continued setting up the last row of chairs. I slung the guitar strap over my shoulder and tuned my guitar.

"Hey, Captain, can you play *That's Amore*?'

I sat down and played the opening notes of the song, then sang the first verse, in my best Dean Martin imitation. A few people joined in the chorus as the room started to fill.

The residents loved hearing the songs of their youth and our sing-alongs were some of the most popular events. *Jailhouse Rock*, a female voice called from the back of the room.

I strummed the chords and sang the opening, a dozen voices joining in as I hit the middle of the first verse. We sang the second verse and the last chord echoed in the room. The back door banged open and Wendy swept into the room in her wench costume. The top covered all her tattoos, and the mid-calf, ragged skirt was more modest than her usual business dress. She'd teased her hair so it was wild, and the dark makeup around her eyes made her look ominous, almost zombie-like. She cackled as she pranced down the side of the room and swept up to me.

"Are we ready to sing some pirate songs?"

The crowd laughed and cheered, "Yes!"

She leaned down and whispered, *Dead Man's Chest*, to me.

"Okay! You people on the left, you're going to sing, 'yo ho ho.' And the right, you're going to sing, 'and a bottle of rum.'" Let's practice.

I strummed the opening as Wendy sang, "Fifteen men on a dead man's chest."

She pointed left and the crowd sang, "Yo ho ho."

She pointed right and they sang, "And a bottle of rum."

We sang three verses and the crowd got into it, each side trying to outdo the other half of the room. We finished and the residents were clapping and laughing. Miriam wheeled a cart through the door and Wendy rushed to her side.

"Arrr matey Miriam has the grog! Who'd like a cup of grog?"

Wendy and Miriam distributed the small plastic cups, each garnished with a wedge of lime.

I blanked on another pirate song, so I started playing *Ghost Riders in the Sky*. The residents clapped along and passed the cups of grog down the rows. I wondered about the ratio of rum and mix we were serving to the dozens of senior citizens who weren't fleet of foot even when totally sober. No one snorted when they tasted the grog, so I assumed it was adequately dilute.

I played *Folsom Prison Blues*, as the last cups of grog were passed to the front rows. Wendy joined me in the last verse. Miriam handed me a cup of grog and I held it up to the crowd and tipped it back.

I felt a tug at my waist and I heard the sword slide out of the scabbard while my head was tipped back. Halfway through a swallow, I choked, getting a roar from the crowd. I looked at Wendy, who was swinging the sword around like a drunken pirate. She winked at me, and I knew her revenge was upon me.

"All right! We're going to sing 'Drunken Sailor.' The left side will sing 'Way hey,' and the right side sings, 'And up she rises.'"

We ran through it a couple times, Wendy pointing the sword toward the left and right sides when it was their turn to sing. The first verse went well. "Way hey, and up she rises," going well, if a little out of synch.

She and I sang the second verse, "Shave his belly with a rusty razor..." with Wendy swinging the sword over her head and pacing behind me. I tried to keep her in sight and ducked a couple times when the sword swooped over my head, bringing roars from the people, who thought it was a well-rehearsed comedy routine.

Wendy pointed the sword left and the crowd sang, "Way hey!" She pointed right and got, "And up she rises!" with everyone joining in on "Early in the morning."

We sang, "Put him in bed with the captain's daughter," as Wendy drifted far to the right, still slinging the sword over her head. We were approaching the chorus when Wendy took a great swoop with the sword and a ripping sound froze her. The left drape hung in the air for a second, then slowly crumpled and fell as the lower portion was sliced away. Wendy stopped singing, and watched it fall, turning ashen.

The residents thought it was part of the show and laughed. I kept singing and led them into the chorus, then into the next verse, "Put him in the longboat 'till he's sober…" Wendy lowered the sword and stared silently at the heap of drapery. She sheepishly carried the sword to me, laying it on the floor next to my stool.

She leaned close. "I didn't know it was sharp."

"Keep singing."

We sang the final chorus of the song and everyone joined in.

Wendy looked at the drape on the floor and whispered, "Nancy's going to kill me. Why didn't you warn me the sword was sharp?"

"I never took it out of the scabbard." I looked to the crowd, who were awaiting the next song. "Any requests?"

"Elvis!" A voice in the rear yelled.

I strummed *Love me Tender* and Wendy joined in, much more subdued than she'd been before the drapes fell.

We sang three more songs. Wendy recovered her composure and announced the costume competition. Only three men attempted a pirate look and one of those relied on three-days beard growth as his costume. Six women came forward, three with bandanas wrapped around their heads and one who'd teased her hair and darkened her eyes. None of the costumes were much more than dark pants and tattered t-shirts for the men. The women were a little more wench-like with long skirts and peasant blouses. Dolores' costume was among the best.

Wendy stood behind each man, holding her hand over their heads while the crowd voted by clapping. Bill Pierce won, thanks to his eye patch.

Next came the voting for the women. The vote was close and so we narrowed it to two finalists, Louanna Rice and Jeri Westfall. Louanna had darkened eyes and sultry wench look, but Jeri's costume, with peasant blouse and long skirt was very well done. Wendy stood behind each of them, urging the crowd on, and in the end declaring a tie. We took pictures of all the contestants, to be posted on the bulletin board. Judy, the café owner, donated $5 gift certificates, enough to cover the cost of coffee and a pastry, and the winners were beaming as they accepted their prize.

With the contest over, Wendy helped Miriam gather the cups. I carefully put the sword back into the scabbard and carried my guitar to the back of the room where the winners were being congratulated. People patted my shoulder as they shook hands With Louanna, Jerri, and Bill, then filed out.

Howard Johnson stopped next to me and leaned close. "I thought we handled the grog pretty well. Wendy and I sampled it and decided diluting it three-parts water to one-part rum was about right. It still tasted like rum, but each person only got a half ounce of rum in a glass." He paused and watched Wendy picking up cups from the floor. "Wendy may have sampled quite a few dilutions before we got the ratio right."

"Do you think that may have contributed to the drapery incident?"

Howard's eyes sparkled. "I'd say she was probably more uninhibited than usual."

"She must've had more than a little diluted rum."

Howard raised his eyebrows. "There was a bit left after we filled all the glasses and Wendy didn't want it to be wasted."

Nancy walked into the room, all smiles. "It sounded like your program was a hit. I could hear the choruses of the pirate songs all the way to my office."

"The residents really got into it."

Howard nodded. "The grog was a nice touch, even if no one got enough to get tipsy."

Nancy eventually noticed the missing piece of drapery and looked at the fabric on the floor. "What on earth?"

"There was a scenery malfunction," Howard said, patting her arm and leaving without explanation.

Nancy looked at me, her question unspoken.

"Um, Wendy didn't know the sword was sharp."

"What?"

"She was leading the chorus and got carried away. The tip of the sword nicked the drape."

Wendy was quietly following Miriam and the cart of empty cups out the door. Nancy drew a breath, glared at me, then followed them down the hallway.

Bingle was in the back of the room, ready to stow the chairs. He put his hand on my shoulder. "I don't think Wendy will try to get even with you for a long time."

* * *

I went back to my office and changed out of my costume. I set the scabbard in the corner next to the guitar, trying to decide how to deal with the razor-sharp blade. It was not going to be a good thing to have laying around the house with Jeremy and a toddler.

"What happens if you take the P out of pirate?"

Brian dropped into my chair before I could even look up.

"He gets irate."

"I thought you were saving your pirate jokes for the contest."

Brian looked surprised. "The entries closed an hour ago. The judges are reading

168

them now and the winner will be announced tomorrow."

"Already?"

"You do know tomorrow is Saturday. I hope you've been practicing your piccolo solo." He handed me a stack of sheet music. "Here are the rest of the songs the band is going to play. John says he'd like you to play the flute, if that's okay."

I took a deep breath. *Crap, I haven't even found the piccolo yet and I have no idea where the flute is*. "Thanks for bringing the music."

Brian glanced at the scabbard with the ivory sword handle sticking out. "That looks like scrimshaw on a real ivory handle. Are you trying to win the costume contest?"

"I'm not planning to enter."

"A sword like that might give you an edge!" Brian laughed. "Get it? A sharp sword giving you an edge."

I smiled. "Very clever."

Brian hopped up, his cherubic smile broke my dark mood, and I involuntarily grinned. "See you tomorrow, Doc."

Brian's aura barely cleared the room when Jenny walked in and sat in the same chair. "I got confirmation that my costume was delivered this afternoon." When I didn't immediately respond, Jenny leaned forward. "What's the matter?"

"Did you hear about the drapes in the community room?"

"What about them?"

"Wendy was swinging my sword around while leading a song chorus and she cut them down."

Jenny's eyes widened and darted to the scabbard. "The sword is sharp?"

"Apparently."

"Does Nancy know?"

I nodded. "She came in shortly after the incident."

Dolores' head popped around the doorframe. "You looked good in the pirate costume."

"I should've checked the sword to see if it was sharp before I brought it here."

"It's been in the basement for decades and I didn't recall ever seeing it out of the scabbard, so I couldn't have warned you."

Jenny nodded toward the scabbard. "You said the handle looks like real ivory."

Dolores considered Jenny's words. "I'm sure the handle is ivory and silver. I think the sword and scabbard are probably very valuable. You should have them appraised and insured."

"They're yours, Dolores."

She shook her head. "Everything I left in the house belongs to you. Do with it as you see fit."

Jenny frowned. "But they're your memories."

"I'm making new friends and new memories here." With that, she left.

Jenny glanced at the sword. "Where could you get it appraised?"

I thought for a second and remembered Meg's shop. "I can take it to the antiques shop. Meg might be able to determine the value. I'll stop off on my way home."

With some difficulty, Jenny stood. "Why don't you leave it with her while she does the appraisal? I don't want something sharp enough to cut down drapes anywhere near Jeremy and his curious friends."

I carried the costume and sword under my arm as I cut through the lobby. Margaret closed her mailbox, then waved at me. I was tempted to pretend I didn't see her, but Alison, the receptionist, called my name. I turned and Alison pointed to Margaret, who was making her way slowly toward me.

"Peter! Peter!" She got to me, winded from her walk across the lobby. "I remember where Collie lived."

I waited for Margaret to catch her breath. "Take a second."

She put her hand on my arm. "She's from that state that starts with C, M, or V."

"Connecticut, Massachusetts, Vermont, or Maine?"

"Yes! That's it!"

"Which?"

"One of those."

I looked at my watch, hoping Margaret caught the hint that I wanted to leave. "You check her record. I think she was arrested for killing her parents."

"If she'd killed her parents, she'd be in prison."

"Well…if I told you she'd been arrested for speeding, you wouldn't check on her."

"Was she arrested for speeding?"

"I can't remember, but it was a big deal. I think it was in the newspapers and everything. One of her aunts told me about it at Artie's wedding."

"If she was ever arrested, I'm sure it was for something minor, like shoplifting, when she was a kid. She's not a criminal."

Margaret didn't like that reply. "You mark my words, that woman killed Artie!"

A crowd gathered around us and I tried to end the rumor that was about to explode. "Colleen West is a respected hard-working lady who's not a killer. Please don't tell people she's a killer."

Margaret stuck her finger in my face. "She is no lady. She bought that sailboat, and she went out with some man. No *lady* sails alone with someone who's not her husband."

I pulled Margaret aside. "Who told you she was sailing with someone other than Art?"

"My sister. Art told Christine that he was too busy to sail as much as Collie wanted to. She has a male 'friend' who sails with her when Artie's busy."

"Please don't spread that rumor around here. It'll only inflame things."

"It's not a rumor! Artie told his mother about it." Margaret stalked off.

Chapter Eight

Meg's shop was busier than I'd ever seen it with eight people roaming the aisles. Meg was haggling with a woman over the price of a glass-based kerosene lamp when I approached the counter. She acknowledged me with a nod, but never stopped her negotiation.

I walked to a section of counter with estate jewelry and marveled at the beautiful old settings. They were probably from the days when ship captains and mine owners lived in large houses, giving their wives expensive baubles for Christmas. I wondered if there was much market for the items displayed. Meg's negotiation reached a conclusion, and she wrapped the lamp and glass chimney carefully in paper before packing them in a box.

She checked on the other customers, who were still searching her stock. Then she returned to me. "What's up, Peter?"

I held up the sword and scabbard. "I'd like to know what this is worth."

She took the scabbard and carried it to the counter near the cash register. She turned the scabbard end to end, then studied the handle and knights-head hilt. "This isn't a cheap replica."

"My friend said it's been in her basement for decades. The last time she remembered seeing it was for a costume party in the

1930s." I paused. "Be careful. It's razor sharp."

Meg carefully drew the sword as a couple walked up behind me. "The etching on the blade is Templar."

I frowned. "Like Knights Templar?"

"A lot of the early Freemason history is linked to the Templars. There's a school of thought that the Masons and Shriners organizations evolved from the Knights Templar, although there's another school of thought that says the Templars were all killed in France after the kings of Spain and France borrowed from them. It was apparently more expedient to steal the rest of the Templars' riches and kill them off than to repay the loans."

The middle-aged bald man who'd been behind me stepped forward. "That'd be a great addition to my pirate costume. What do you want for it?"

I looked at Meg, who shook her head imperceptibly. "I'm not sure what it's worth."

"I'll give you a hundred dollars."

I was ready to accept when Meg shook her head again. "This is a museum piece. It's worth at least ten times that."

The man shook his head. "That's too rich for my blood." He and his wife returned to their shopping.

I leaned forward. "Really? A thousand dollars?"

Meg shrugged. "That's where I'd start negotiations. I'm sure I could get at least eight hundred for it on the internet. Maybe more if I got it into an east coast auction house."

She took out a magnifying glass and examined the blade. "It was made in Toledo. That increases the value."

"Because it's from Ohio?"

Meg drew a breath and let it out. "Spain. Toledo was the source of the best European swords for hundreds of years. It's too bad this didn't belong to someone famous, like Oscar Wilde or Benjamin Franklin."

I must've snorted. "What are the odds of Benjamin Franklin's Templar sword arriving in a Two Harbors antiques shop?"

"I always hope. The name etched on the blade is A. H. Thomas. I'll do a search, but I assume he's not particularly famous." She slid the sword back into the scabbard and passed it across the counter to me. "I'd like to make an offer if you decide to sell it."

"I'm not ready to sell it, but I don't want it around my young son. Do you take consignments?"

"60:40?"

"Who gets the sixty?" I asked.

"I do. I have to cover my overhead and it might take up counter space for years before it sells."

"How about 40:60, since you think it's valuable and you'll make hundreds when it sells?"

Meg pulled the sword back and wrote a receipt for me. "This is in case I croak or go bankrupt. You can prove you own it."

I shook her hand and was about to turn away. "Do you have any muzzle-loading pistols?"

She shook her head. "Not right now. I can keep an eye out for one if you're in the market."

"Have you sold one recently?"

"Not in years. They're not rare, but people don't just walk in with one every week."

"Who bought the last one?"

"I don't recall. I've sold a lot of stuff since then."

"Do you network with other dealers?"

"Sure, we call back and forth when a customer is looking for something specific."

"Call around and find out if anyone's sold a black-powder pistol recently."

Meg looked up as the entrance bell dinged. Two more customers walked in. "I can make some calls Monday. I need to deal with my paying customers right now."

I nodded as the phone rang. Meg picked it up, but immediately put her finger into the air to catch my attention. "Yes, Chief. You're set for tomorrow. Thanks." She hung up and smiled. "The firemen will position a fire truck up the hill from the park, ready to flush the street after the lutefisk throw."

"I thought there were pollution concerns. You know, washing toxic waste into the lake."

Meg smiled. "The chamber discussed it and decided lutefisk is dead fish and there are already lots of dead fish in Lake Superior. Clancy Reynolds said the seagulls will gobble it up like candy."

"It's soaked in lye."

"The lye is rinsed out."

"Don't say I didn't warn you if there's a fish kill or if the seagulls start dying."

Meg waved off my concerns. "I heard you were a glass half-empty kind of guy."

"I think of myself as a realist."

Meg laughed. "Try being a shop owner in a town with a three-month tourist season and then talk to me about being a realist."

* * *

I beat Jenny home and found the cardboard box with Jenny's pirate costume still on the steps. Jeremy was finishing a peanut butter sandwich and doing homework in the dining room.

"Why didn't you carry the box in when you came home?"

"What box?"

"The one on the back steps."

"I didn't see it."

"You must've moved it to get in the door."

He shrugged. "I don't remember."

"We're having chili for supper."

Jeremy's eyes lit up. "With muffins and honey?"

"Sure. I'll whip up some cornmeal muffins and pop them in the oven."

The aroma of muffins filled the kitchen by the time Jenny got home. I was washing the mixing bowl and she greeted me with a peck on the cheek. "Whatever is in the oven smells wonderful."

"They'll be ready when you've changed."

I was taking the muffins out of the tin when Jeremy rushed in. "Mom yelled for you."

I set the hot muffin pan aside and rushed upstairs. Jenny was standing in front of the full-length mirror modeling her pirate costume. She ran her hand over her baby bump. "The T-shirt is really snug."

I laughed "It's really cute."

She sighed and rested her head on my shoulder. "I'm tired of being pregnant and it's all your fault."

"I thought we wanted a baby."

"It's easy for you to say. You did the fun part. I'm the one who's waddling around like I'm pregnant with a baby elephant." She punched my shoulder for emphasis.

"I just pulled the muffins out of the oven. Let's eat while they're still warm."

I helped Jenny pull the pirate shirt over her head. She ran her fingers through her hair and followed me downstairs.

Jeremy was setting the table with salad plates, bowls, spoons, the muffins, butter knives, and butter. He sat in his spot with the squeeze bottle of honey in his hand. "Can we eat?"

"I'll get the chili," I said as he dove into the pile of muffins.

We were clearing the table when my cellphone rang. "Hello."

"Peter, I need your help tomorrow morning."

I recognized Meg's distinctive voice. "I thought things were under control?"

"For the most part, they are. But Ed Gardner's wife called. He's just had an appendectomy and I need to replace him."

"I'm..."

"Please. I'm really in a pinch. He was going to help load the morning naturist cruise at ten, and he's scheduled to judge the pirate costume contest at one."

"My wife is pregnant, and I don't want to leave her alone with my son."

"Please..."

I walked back to the dining room where Jeremy was buttering his third muffin. "Meg Cochran is on the phone and she wants me to help downtown tomorrow morning."

Jenny scooped up a spoonful of chili. "Go. I'd planned to hang around the house with Jeremy until the afternoon. He and I will go to the sidewalk art contest and children's face painting. Take your cellphone and I'll call if I need you."

I paced between the living room and kitchen as we spoke. "Meg, I've got permission to abandon the family until the band concert."

"Great! Go right to the historical society building, and we'll sort out who's going where with whom. And Peter, wear your pirate costume."

I sighed. "Yeah."

"The bicorn hat, too."

"Sure."

"Peter," Jenny called from the dining room.

I held the phone aside. "What do you need?"

"Have you found the piccolo yet?"

I closed my eyes. "I was just going to look for it."

"Take Jeremy with you."

I ended my call with Meg.

Jeremy talked about Jacob Stone like he was the source of all the world's wisdom. I was pleased because I knew the Stones were a nice family and Jacob was a polite, smart kid who behaved in school and at home.

Jeremy followed me upstairs after we'd cleared the table. "Where are we going to look?"

"I think it's near the accordion."

"Cool! Will you play the accordion for me?"

"Focus. I need to find a little flat black case with a piccolo." Then I pinched my eyes shut remembering the piccolo wasn't the only instrument I needed for the concert. "And a larger flat case with a flute."

I pulled out drawers in the cabinets lining Dolores' display room. The shelves were filled with Hummels, milk-glass eggs, china dolls, and other collectibles. Jeremy dug into boxes we hadn't unloaded in the hubbub of preparing for Christmas and the arrival of the baby.

"Is this it?" Jeremy asked, holding up the piccolo case.

"Yes. Is the flute in that box too?"

Jeremy rattled in the box, making me hope all the breakables had been removed. He stood up with the flute case in one hand. "I think so." He flipped the latches before I could stop him, and flute pieces spilled on the floor and into the box. "Oops."

We got the pieces back into the case and carried the two instruments to my bedroom. I assembled the piccolo and tuned it to ear. Then I played the *Stars and Stripes Forever* piccolo solo from memory, missing a few notes the first time through. The second time went perfectly, Jeremy watching as if in a trance."

"That was good, Dad."

I put the piccolo back into the case and assembled the flute, relieved the pieces were undamaged. Then I rethought the assessment. If they'd been damaged, I wouldn't have to play with the band.

Jeremy misunderstood my sigh of resignation. "Is it broken?"

"It's fine." I blew a few notes, tuned it, then set it on the dresser. "I have sheets of music in the car. Please run down and bring them back here."

"Can't you do it?"

"You can listen to me practice."

He nodded with resignation and left for the car. I held up Jenny's pirate t-shirt and laughed.

Jeremy rushed in with the sheet music and handed it to me. "Do you have to learn all these songs tonight?"

I flipped through the music. "I don't need to memorize them, only practice them so I can play them tomorrow." I set a few sheets on a chair and Jeremy watched as I played the flute part of a couple Sousa marches.

When I switched sheets he stood. "I thought you were going to play songs I knew."

"Those are songs you'll recognize when you hear the whole band play them, but listening only to the flute part doesn't give you the entire melody or harmony."

"It's boring, Dad."

"I've got to play the rest of these, then I'll be downstairs."

Jeremy took a step, then turned back. "Mom is watching those movies on the TV that make her cry. Can I play a computer game?"

"Sure."

* * *

Damp tissues were spread around Jenny on the couch. On television, the happy couple were climbing into the back of a limo as snowflakes swirled around them. Another sappy Christmas miracle brought Jenny to tears.

"Why do you watch those goofy movies?"

"Because..." sniffle "they make me" honk "feel good." She wiped her eyes and set another damp tissue on the pile.

I sat next to her. "But you always cry."

She nodded. "Tears of happiness."

Jeremy was playing something on an iPad in the dining room. He shut the screen abruptly when I approached, so I assumed it was something we didn't approve of. I didn't see any point in berating him since he acted guilty before I could speak.

"Time for bed."

"Dad," he sighed, "tomorrow is Saturday. I don't have to get up for school."

"I don't want your sleep pattern to get messed up on the weekend. That just makes Monday morning more difficult."

"But Monday isn't for two more days."

"Put your pajamas on and brush your teeth."

He got up and set the iPad on the table. "Can we have popcorn after I put my pajamas on?"

Jenny was listening from the other room. "Popcorn sounds good."

"Pajamas, then popcorn."

He bounded up the stairs and I found a box of microwave popcorn in the pantry. Jeremy was back in the kitchen before the microwave dinged. "Can I have my own bowl?"

I took two mixing bowls down and filled a small one for Jeremy, who took it into the living room. Moving aside some damp tissues, I sat next to Jenny, who'd found a 1950s comedy on an obscure cable channel.

"Things were so much simpler back then," I whispered to her as Abbott and Costello tried to escape from the invisible man.

She took a handful of popcorn and put some into her mouth. "No drugs, no swearing, no one getting shot. Just slapstick humor."

Jeremy was on the edge of his seat, watching the comedy duo ducking through an old mansion, trying to escape the specter they couldn't see, but who was slamming doors and moving furniture.

"I wonder if this will give him nightmares?" I whispered.

Jenny looked away from the television and met my gaze. "It's no worse than our Christmas ghost."

"And he spent several nights in our bed through that ordeal."

She put her hand on my thigh and rubbed it. "I suppose it might upset him. You'll be sleeping in his bed, just like when you had broken ribs and the doctor told you to refrain from bedroom gymnastics."

"We couldn't consummate our marriage."

Jenny grinned and patted her stomach. "You planted this seed a couple weeks before the wedding. I think that counts."

I kissed her as Jeremy set his empty popcorn bowl on the coffee table, his eyes glued to the television as the comedians ran from the mansion.

"Bedtime, buddy."

"Dad, they're just escaping from the invisible man. We've got to see if they make it!"

Jenny's stomach was jiggling as she stifled her laughing. I knew I'd lost, so we watched the end. The credits started rolling. "They're safe. You can go to bed now."

I followed Jeremy upstairs and watched him brush his teeth. In bed, he looked at me earnestly and asked, "Why wasn't that movie in color?"

"They didn't have color movies back then."

"Why not?"

"Color movie film hadn't been invented yet."

He stared at me, deep in thought. "Why?"

"I don't know. There were movies made a long time ago that didn't even have sound."

He cocked his head. "That'd be boring."

"They wrote the dialog on the screen so you could read what they were saying."

He snuggled under the covers. "Like subtitles in Japanese cartoons?"

"Yeah, kind of like that."

The sound of Jenny's footsteps came upstairs and light switches clicked. I ducked into the bathroom and brushed my teeth. She'd was already in bed when I turned off the bedroom lights.

"I want this baby to come early. I'm ready to be skinny again."

I put my dirty clothes into the hamper and spooned into her back. "The timing isn't our choice."

She sighed. "I know."

Chapter Nine

Jenny had been up many times during the night, so I slipped out of bed, shaved, and changed clothes in the bathroom. I left the house before either she or Jeremy woke up. I stopped at Judy's and ate breakfast while reading the newspaper.

Kerry Stone pulled out a chair next to me and sat, signaling the waitress for coffee. "I see you're ready for the festival." He nodded toward the hat with ostrich plume sitting on the chair next to me.

"I guess."

"Why are you in town so early?"

"Meg called and asked me to help load people onto the sunbathing cruise. She also needed a replacement judge for the costume contest."

Kerry's coffee arrived and he watched the waitress retreat, waiting until she was out of earshot. "I've got nothing on the murder. No one saw anything or anyone in the harbor. The only fingerprints on the boat were from the victim and his wife with an odd set under the cabinet that's probably from the guy who did the original wiring when the boat was built."

"Did someone check on the purchase of antique guns and equipment for casting lead balls."

"Hundreds of internet sites sell either old or replica black powder pistols or kits to assemble one. Anyone can have one delivered to his door. There's no recordkeeping requirements, and none of the suppliers were willing to tell us if they'd shipped a gun here without a subpoena."

"I asked Meg if she'd sold any at the antiques store. There was a sale long ago, but she couldn't remember who'd bought the gun. She's going to call her network of antiques dealers next week to see if any of them has a recent sale."

"That's an avenue I hadn't considered. I checked pawn shops from here to Cloquet, but none of them sold a black powder pistol recently." Kerry sipped his coffee in silence. "I hope there's not some pirate wandering the festival with a loaded pistol."

"How would we know?" I asked. "It's not like it'd look any different from other pirate pistols."

"That scares the hell out of me."

"Speaking of pistols, I've got a problem."

Kerry cocked his head. "A pistol problem?"

"I found a muzzle-loading pistol in a steamer trunk. It was buried under the uniform."

"A real muzzle-loading pistol?"

"A loaded muzzle-loading pistol."

Kerry glanced around to make sure no one was listening. "What are you going to do with it?"

"First of all, I want to unload it."

"That sounds like a good plan. And..."

"How do you unload a muzzleloader?"

Kerry picked up his coffee and took a sip while considering the question. "I suppose you have to fire it."

"There's got to be another way."

"Well, you can't drill out the ball. Black powder is unstable, and you might ignite it with the drill. I think the safest thing to do is fire it into soft dirt."

"There isn't a cap on the firing nipple. I don't have a way of firing it."

Kerry smiled. "With a curious boy in the house, that's probably a good thing." He thought for a moment. "Edgar, my afternoon officer, hunts deer with a muzzleloader. I'll ask him if I can have a cap. We can take it outside of town and shoot it in a swampy area."

"That's another question. Is it safe to fire?"

"If it's not corroded, it should be as safe to fire as when it was put into storage."

I set the paper aside. "The band is playing *The 1812 Overture*. We can have the pirates shoot their pistols into the air during the finale."

"What would that do?" Kerry asked. Then he froze. "If someone shot a ball into

190

the air, it could kill a person in the crowd when it came down."

"That's my point. I think a guy with a loaded gun wouldn't shoot it in the air. He'd either keep the gun tucked in his belt, or he'd sneak out of the crowd so no one would notice he wasn't shooting his pistol."

Kerry shook his head. "I don't think a killer would do that."

"What have you got to lose?"

"I think it's a harebrained idea. Why would the killer have his gun loaded with a bullet?"

"He's already shot one person; maybe he'll have the gun loaded to protect himself."

Kerry stared at the floor, at a loss for a comeback, but obviously not bought in to my plan.

"Have you got something better?" I asked.

Kerry scratched his neck and wrinkled his nose. "No."

"I'll set it up with the band director."

Kerry stood, but paused before turning toward the door. "I can't believe our best bet for solving a murder rests on a killer not wanting to shoot his gun in the air."

I thought about Margaret Pearson's comments and smiled. "Well, there's one more thing."

Kerry cocked his head. "You're grinning."

"Art West's aunt is convinced Colleen killed him."

"And you don't think she's credible?"

"We've had several conversations, and Margaret thinks North Carolina is in New England. The next time she told me Colleen moved from some state with the word new in its name. Later she said it was M, C, and V states."

The unscarred part of Kerry's face curled into a smile. "You've got some challenging people at your place."

I mopped syrup with the last piece of pancake and popped it in my mouth. "You could say that."

Kerry waved. "Good luck with the costume contest."

"Um, Kerry. Margaret did have one thing that might be credible. She said Colleen is no lady because she goes sailing with some man other than her husband."

Kerry looked around to see if anyone heard me. "The aunt thinks Colleen is cheating on him?"

"I told you what I heard. I didn't extrapolate to infidelity." Margaret's other accusation popped into my head. "The aunt also said Colleen has a record back home, wherever that is. One of Colleen's relatives told her at their wedding."

"Do you think she really remembered that conversation?"

"A lot of the residents recall things from the past better than recent events. That could be the case here."

"Did the Aunt remember why Colleen was arrested?"

"She didn't remember. I blew her off by suggesting Colleen may have been arrested for shoplifting candy as a kid."

Kerry stared at his shoes while shaking his head. "Len said you did a good job of filtering rumors before feeding him information. This sounds pretty sketchy."

I wiped my mouth and stood up. "You said you were out of ideas..."

"I am, but I don't need to be chasing wild hares. Especially when the source isn't sure where North Carolina is located."

"Hey, to her credit, Margaret said Colleen was from out east before she said New England."

"So which is it, out east or New England?"

I looked at my bill and set cash on the table. "It's one of those states that starts with north, new, M, C, or V."

Kerry glared at me. "Oh yeah, I can see how you were a big help to Len. I think he suggested you just for comic relief."

* * *

Walking past the park on my way to the historical society building, I encountered a dozen people scouring every corner, apparently searching for the hidden medallion. A husband and wife team were moving a ladder from tree to tree. The wife held the ladder while the husband checked branches and knot holes for the medallion. They had obviously taken to heart the first clue that said, "look high and low."

I was amazed that two men, wearing rubber gloves, had dumped out a waste can and were pawing through every piece of paper and food scrap. I stopped to watch and one of them looked up. "Don't worry, we'll put it all back in the garbage can."

"Did I miss a clue that mentioned garbage?"

The younger man looked at me suspiciously. "Are you a treasure hunter?"

"I'm helping load the tour boat and judging the costume contest."

Assessing me as no risk, he dug a scrap of paper out of his pocket.

For a Swede it's jordnötssmör
The Finns call it maapähkinävoi
They eat it on leipää or bröd
Americans like it as PB&J

Confusion must've shown on my face. The older man, perhaps the father, leaned close and whispered. "We're looking for a peanut butter sandwich."

I don't brag, but my pirate costume was the best among those worn by volunteers at the historical society. A majority of the volunteers were wenches, mostly wrapped in sweaters to fend off the breeze sweeping off Lake Superior and into Two Harbors.

Meg Cochran made no attempt at piracy in her costume. Wearing a blue sweatshirt with a logo of the Two Harbors lighthouse, she was all business. "Listen up! I've got you all assigned to critical tasks that have to begin before the tourists swamp us." She handed out sheets of paper. The left column was an alphabetical list of the volunteers, and the right column was a list of tasks. The back was an agenda of the day's events with their locations. Meg was organized.

After a short question and answer period, we split up for our assignments. I smelled the sausage cooking for the Rotary club breakfast in the park as I exited the city museum. A fire truck drove by as I walked to the harbor where a passenger boat gently rose and fell with the lake swells.

A bearded middle-aged man, wearing a seaman's sweater and captain's cap was standing next to the gangway speaking with a young woman wrapped in a long coat. They were deep in discussion when I approached.

"I'm Peter, here to help with crowd control when your passengers board."

The captain smiled and turned to me. "I'm Captain Jack and this is my daughter and first mate, Addie." His handshake was firm, and his hands were calloused, a man who worked hard for a living. In contrast, Addie's handshake was limp, her hands as cold as a fish fresh out of Lake Superior.

I looked around. "It doesn't look like there's much crowd to control."

Jack checked his watch again, a large silver chronometer that looked like something a pilot would wear. "The busload of naturists will be here in five minutes. The rest of the passengers should be close behind."

"There really are nudists coming for the trip?" I asked.

"This is one of their monthly trips. They book my boat for the second Saturday in June, July, August, and September every year."

Addie nodded. "They're our most dependable group. They're polite, not drunk, not rowdy, and they tip well."

"I have a hard time visualizing naked people cruising Lake Superior."

Jack shrugged. "One of the women told me they were hardy Minnesotans taking advantage of the few months of summer."

Addie nodded. "I've got pictures if…"

I put up my hands, not interested in seeing naked bodies turning blue in the cold Lake Superior air. "I believe you."

A school bus turned at the stoplight and drove toward us. Jack checked is watch again. "That's probably them."

I must've looked apprehensive because Addie smiled. "Don't worry, they usually arrive in bathrobes and beach coverups. They don't disrobe until we're away from shore."

I let out an involuntary sigh as the bus rolled to a stop. Stepping to the door, I put my hand out to help a middle-aged woman step down from the bus. As Addie said, she was wrapped in a heavy terrycloth robe. The woman was followed by a similarly wrapped man who was probably her husband. The naturists unloaded, all polite and smiling. None were the hard-bodied teens Hulda was expecting to see on the trip. The youngest couple was my age, mid-thirties.

Addie greeted the customers like old friends and helped them across the gangway. With the last aboard, she stepped over to me. "You were expecting Playboy bunnies."

The truth in her statement caught me off guard. "I didn't know what to expect."

A few other couples were walking toward us after parking around the museum. All wore some type of robe or coverup, carrying towels and carryon bags. The

197

Whistling Pines van turned the corner as Addie helped a foursome over the gangway.

Wearing a flowered housecoat, Hulda Packer was the first person off the van. Her black orthopedic shoes seemed out of place after seeing the naturists arriving in flip-flops and white boating shoes. I'd never seen Hulda's legs in anything but heavy support hose, and the sight of her bulging purple varicose veins and the white sagging skin above her knees was something I wouldn't soon forget.

She looked around. "Where are the nudes?"

"The naturists' bus just unloaded. They're already on the boat."

Hulda tottered past me, and Addie helped her across the gangway. Considering she usually used a walker, Hulda shuffled along pretty well.

Ginny Johnson was next off the bus, wearing dark slacks and a pullover sweater. I was surprised that she'd joined the cruise of naturists. She sensed my confusion. "I'm just along for the boat ride. I really don't care if the others are naked or dressed."

I nodded and passed her on to Addie.

The next half-dozen passengers were a mix of people coming to enjoy a boat ride and folks in bathrobes or housecoats who were apparently prepared to sunbathe. That is, until we got to Alma Kotter, a relatively new resident more affluent than most of the others and given to a spark of mischievousness. She's pranked a couple of the health aides delivering her daily meds, and routinely had the people at her dining table laughing over tales of her antics as a young woman. I helped her down the steps, watching her sandals, and noting the hem of a fur coat.

I glanced up at the full-length fur, then saw Alma's grin. My guard went up, but I smiled back. "That's a lovely fur. Is it mink?"

"It's just like the one Ava Gardner wore when she pranked Frank Sinatra."

My mind rushed through film history and I recalled hearing a story about Ava walking up to Sinatra in a mink coat, pulling it open, and exposing her naked body. My recollection process took a second too long, and I was unable to intervene before Alma opened the coat. I turned my head, seeing only a flash of thigh. I heard snickering from Wendy, who was behind Alma. A round of applause came from the boat.

"What's the matter Peter. Are you shy?" Alma asked.

I opened my mouth but was out of witty quips. "I'm trying to maintain a professional relationship with the residents. That includes not exposing our nude bodies to each other."

"I have a professional relationship with my doctor, and he's seen me naked." She paused. "You can turn around now. I'm covered."

I turned. Like Alma, Wendy, who was on the van's steps, had a broad smile. I offered my hand to Alma. "Let me help you to the gangway."

Wendy stepped down and handed me the keys. "Will you park the van? Leave the keys at the historical society and I'll pick them up when we return."

Wendy was wearing a beach coverup that exposed her bare legs. My eyes were drawn to the rose tattoo on her right calf. "I thought Nancy didn't want any new tattoos exposed to the residents."

Wendy shook her head. "It's just a rose on a stem and it's on my calf. People have seen it when I've worn a skirt or dress."

I took the keys from her. "And there aren't any other surprises under your coverup?"

Her eyes sparkled and she reached for the bow tying the top. "Are you the tattoo inspector?"

I grabbed her hand before she untied the bow. "I'm not inspecting anything. Get on the boat and remember Nancy considers us Whistling Pines ambassadors."

Wendy's Cheshire cat smile always unnerved me. "I assure you that everything I do will reflect well on Whistling Pines."

I drove the van away, catching a glimpse of Wendy untying her coverup and modeling a one-piece bathing suit in the van's mirror.

Addie seemed impressed with either the suit or a tattoo; I didn't want to know which.

The sun broke through the thin overhead clouds and the breeze calmed as I walked back to the dock. Addie checked off the names of the last few passengers as I returned to the gangway. "That's everyone who's prepaid for a ticket. I'll tell Dad and we'll push off." She stripped off her coverup and laid it over the rail, exposing a skimpy bikini. "Can you untie the front line?"

The shock must've shown on my face. Addie smiled. "Peter, the front line."

"Ah, sure. I've got it."

Addie hopped on the boat and pulled the gangway across. "We'll see you in two hours."

I watched the boat pull away as several naturists shed their covers and laid towels on their seats before sitting down, facing the morning sun. It was one of those moments where being a gentleman and looking away was trumped by my awe at seeing so much bare skin exposed in one place.

Kerry's voice caused me to spin around. "I haven't seen that much skin since I was showering in basic training." He too, was watching the naturists disrobing on the boat.

"There weren't any middle-aged women in Navy basic training."

Kerry nodded and turned toward the park. "Reminds me why I make sure my in-laws aren't using the bathroom before I walk in."

My thoughts turned immediately to Barbara, Jenny's mother. Her dress was always more than modest with never a hint of cleavage or a skirt that exposed even her knees. That was the image of her in my mind, and that's the one I wanted to stay there. "Amen to that," I replied.

I walked to the park with Kerry, who greeted people with a polite nod as they passed. A couple children seemed shocked or intrigued by the burn scars that covered one side of his face and one hand. Their parents were polite and didn't stare.

An out-of-town couple carrying a metal detector met us on the sidewalk. "Excuse us. Do you know if anyone's been over the park with a detector yet?"

I pointed out a man who'd been walking a grid, back and forth through the park, since I'd parked my car. "He's been searching for the medallion all morning."

They nodded and walked toward the lighthouse.

Kerry watched them walk away. "You don't need to talk to John Carr. I saw him unloading his car behind the bandshell and I spoke to him about having the pirates fire their guns. He thought it would be a nice touch."

"Thanks. I'm sure that has more gravity coming from you, the police chief, than if it came from me."

Kerry stared off into the distance, apparently considering something other than the medallion seekers. He took a deep breath and turned back to me. "Thank you."

"For what?"

"For introducing me to Len and getting me out of my cocoon of self pity."

"All I did was invite you out for coffee."

Kerry stopped and turned toward me. "Peter..." he let out a breath. "I was suicidal. You put meaning back into my life. I can't thank you enough."

I was taken aback by his words. "It's what vets do for each other. Vern, the VFW bartender, pulled me out of a deep hole and connected me with Whistling Pines." I paused. "Sometimes we need a nudge to get our lives back on track. I'm glad I could be the one who got you there."

"You're smart and sly." He paused, watching the people as they passed. "This case has me scratching my head. I don't see a motive. Love, jealousy, and money are the usual drivers. I just don't see any of those here. As for opportunity, phew, anyone with access to the marina could've walked or motored out to the sailboat and killed Art."

"It must've been someone he knew."

Kerry raised his one unscarred eyebrow. "Peter, this is a small town. Art went to school with a quarter of the residents and probably knew half the others. Saying it was someone he knew doesn't narrow the suspect list much."

I blew out a breath, seeing the wisdom in his words. "That's why you're the chief and I'm just a lowly musician."

A middle-aged man in a brown sheriff's department uniform approached us. He waved at Kerry to get his attention. "Who's that?"

"I've only seen his picture in the newspaper, but I think it's the Lake County Sheriff."

Shaking hands and smiling, the sheriff was an obvious politician. He spoke to the people nearest us, then put his hand out to Kerry. "Congratulations, Chief Stone. I'm Bud Hamm."

Kerry shook his hand. "This is Peter Rogers, the Whistling Pines Recreation Director."

The sheriff shook my hand and smiled. "Len mentioned your assistance in a couple investigations. I heard you and the Chief were key to solving the mystery of the time capsule."

"Kerry solved that. I was just along when they put the pieces together."

Bud continued to smile, and I was beginning to wonder if a perpetual smile was a requirement for election as sheriff. "Len was laughing so hard he was nearly in tears when he told me about your run-in with the moose in your neighbor's yard. That was…something."

"I don't expect I'll be fending off a moose with a broom ever again."

Nodding, the sheriff turned to Kerry. "Could we talk for a second?" The sheriff looked toward an alley next to the beer garden. "There's a quiet corner over there."

Kerry nodded toward the middle of the park. "I heard you're judging the pirate and wench costume competition. You'd better get over to the bandshell."

I walked to the row of chairs behind a table set in front of the bandshell. There was a notepad and pencil on the table in front of each chair. People started filing into the park from all directions, some continuing the medallion search, while others were lining up for the costume judging.

I introduced myself to the other judges, local business owners, and members of the chamber of commerce. They reintroduced themselves, all having met me at some point during my Two Harbors residence. We chatted about the judging, agreeing that we weren't going to be too serious about the criteria or the final decision.

Meg brought a microphone onto the stage and quieted the crowd. "We'll start the costume contest in a minute. Before we do that, I have a representative from the newspaper who's going to read the winning pirate joke."

A young man who I'd never seen before, walked onto the stage nervously. I leaned to Peggy Mattson, sitting next to me. "Who is he?"

"He's an intern at the newspaper."

"Why is he, rather the editor, reading the winning poem?"

Peggy snorted. "I imagine the editor is being cagey and doesn't want to read it himself."

"Because?"

"I think it might be language the editor doesn't want to say in public or he's afraid of people throwing rotten eggs or rutabagas at him."

I rolled my eyes as the young man composed himself in front of the microphone, unfolding a sheet of paper.

"We had over a hundred submissions and the editorial team read them all. It was a tough call because there were three close finalists. But we all finally agreed this was the best." He cleared his throat and looked at the crowd earnestly. "A pirate walks into a bar with a big ship's wheel jammed in his pants. The bartender asks him, 'Excuse me, but do you know you have a wheel inside your pants?' The pirate replies, 'Aye, it's driving me nuts.'"

A groan arose from the crowd, mostly drowning out the few laughs.

The intern waited for the groans to die out, then leaned toward the mic. "The winning submission was from Burt King of Two Harbors."

I heard a hoot from the rear of the crowd, followed by Brian's distinctive voice. "I've got better tuba jokes than that!"

The crowd noise was growing as Meg took the microphone again. "We're going to start the pirate costume competition in ten minutes. I need all the pirates to come around to the back of the bandshell and line up for the judging. Wenches, we'll judge your costumes as soon as we're through with the pirates."

I heard noise from behind, and the aroma of smoked meats drifted over us.

Meg looked over the crowd at something in the distance. "In case you've been wondering about the sumptuous aroma, two food trucks have just opened behind the Lutheran church. Dan's Smokehouse has brisket and smoked pork sandwiches, and Porky's Sausage Village is serving brats, hotdogs, and hamburgers."

A man scooted on the stage and whispered something to Meg, who'd covered the microphone, then rolled her eyes.

She uncovered the mic, "I was just reminded that Porky's slogan is 'You've never sausage such good bratwurst.'"

A collective groan went through the crowd.

Meg put up her hands. "And, in case you need to wash down your bratwurst, North Star Brewing set up a beer garden in front of their trailer. They've got beer and their famous homemade root beer."

The man who cued the sausage ad rushed out and whispered to Meg again.

She nodded, took a deep breath and switched on the mic. "For you diehard Scandinavians, the Sons of Norway are serving potato sausage and lutefisk behind the bandstand. For those of you who aren't lutefisk fans, be glad the breeze is blowing the lutefisk smell away from us."

That brought more than a few laughs. Candy Mason, who'd just moved to Two Harbors to open a cookware shop, leaned close to me. "What's lutefisk and why is everyone laughing?"

"It's a traditional Scandinavian holiday food made by soaking dried cod in lye."

She grimaced. "That sounds terrible. People actually eat it?"

"I think some hardcore Scandinavians do, but it's becoming less popular with each generation."

"What did Meg mean about the wind blowing the other direction?"

"Lutefisk has a distinctive odor and texture. It's like fish flavored gelatin and the smell is…" I stalled, unable to come up with anything that smelled like lutefisk. "I guess it's just stinky."

"Like rotten fish?"

A woman standing behind us was listening and leaned close. "Rotten fish smells better than lutefisk."

Candy looked at her to see if she was kidding.

The woman shrugged. "My parents made us eat it Christmas Eve. The house stunk of lutefisk until New Year's Day."

Candy looked stricken. "Do they feed it to children?"

The woman squatted down and whispered, "I think it's still legal, but I heard the legislature is considering a law to make feeding lutefisk to any child under twelve a misdemeanor."

The smiling woman stood and stepped away from us. Candy watched her for a second, then she looked at me. "Was she serious?"

"No. People around the region joke a lot about lutefisk. It's an odd tradition, but it's wholesome and safe to eat."

"Does it really taste like fishy gelatin and smell really bad?"

"Yes."

Candy shuddered and grimaced. "I think I'll stick with the bratwurst."

Ole Lundquist turned and glared at us. "Lutefisk is Norwegian soul food."

Candy turned to Ole. "Um...how to you eat it? I mean, it's like eating Jell-O."

Ole smiled. "I like it swimming in butter. It just slides down, like eating a raw oyster."

Candy looked at me. "It slides down your throat?" She shuddered.

"Most people dip it in white sauce and chew it, like eating any piece of fish."

Candy looked unconvinced.

Meg consulted with her team, then returned to the microphone. She checked over her shoulder and waved to a group of pirates standing in the wings. "Here's the first of four groups of pirates."

The costumes were good, but the pirate antics were better. The men strutted out in true pirate fashion, growling at the crowd and snarling "Arrr!" at each other. One pirate drew his sword and poked it at the crowd as if he was fending off boarders.

I conferred with the other judges and decided we were going to pick a finalist out of each group. I walked over to Meg and told her our plan and she nodded.

"Our finalist of this group is number one." He was the snarling, sword-wielding guy and he moved stage right as the next group came out.

The second group was equally menacing and well clad. A guy I'd met at the VFW, who'd lost a leg in Iraq, had fashioned a peg leg from a piece of lumber and thumped onto the stage looking mean. We judges quickly chose Pegleg as the finalist from that group. He and the first pirate snarled at each other as the third wave came onstage.

The guys all looked good, but a man with a thick black beard and tri-corner hat stood out from the rest. His natural beady eyes made my skin crawl, as a good pirate's look should, and we moved him over with the first two finalists.

The fourth group was young, probably high school kids, none of whom held a candle to the menacing look of the previous groups. The judges were hung, knowing that none of this group would be the winner. We signaled to Meg that we'd chosen the meekest, spindly kid out of the group. She shrugged and kept him beside her while calling the other three men back to center stage.

The other judges huddled around me. Candy Mason leaned close to be heard over the taunting pirates and the raucous crowd. "I think we should let the crowd choose."

I looked at the finalists. The angry pirate with beady eyes was glaring at us. "I think that's a wonderful idea. I'm afraid to vote against Blackbeard."

Candy approached the stage and relayed our plan to Meg.

"The judges are deadlocked!" We're going to let the crowd choose the winner. Cheer for your favorite pirate as I hold my hand over each head."

The teen got a smattering of polite applause, and Meg urged him off the stage. Each of the remaining pirates got cheers and clapping, each equal to the others. As far as I could tell, it was a three-way tie.

"Okay folks, the pirates are going to walk the stage one more time, then we're going to have you cheer for your favorite."

Pegleg and the first finalist stalked the stage, taunting the crowd and urging them on. Blackbeard walked quietly back and forth, using a stare that would've frozen the lake. Candy leaned close to me. "His stare is giving me goosebumps."

Meg stood behind each of the pirates, letting the crowd cheer. The decision was more evident this time, with Pegleg the winner. She handed him a small trophy and he smiled and left the stage. Blackbeard lingered, saying something to Meg that drained the color from her face.

She composed herself and announced the wench costume competition. The first group of finalists came onto the stage and we quickly chose a young woman whose tattered dress and wild hair made her look genuinely like a battered wench. The second group was evenly matched, and we chose a middle-aged woman who looked like she would've been a finalist in the pirate competition. The third group was teenagers and again we decided to take a waif-like girl who had no chance against the other finalists, and then came the final group.

They were all in good costumes, but one woman stood out, mostly because of the amount of exposed skin. I immediately thought of Wendy's costume, with the peasant shirt off her shoulders and the slit in the skirt that exposed some thigh. She looked confident and snarled at the crowd, which brought a round of cheers. The judges looked at each other and quietly agreed that she was the finalist from the last group.

Meg gathered the finalists on the stage and congratulated each of them. "Okay, crowd. Vote with your cheers." She moved down the line, holding her hand over the head of the finalists. The crowd cheered, clapped, and hooted as she went down the line. We were left with two finalists, the wench with the somewhat revealing outfit and the wench with the wild hair who looked battered.

Meg escorted the others into the wings and returned to the microphone. "Okay, let's have a tie breaking vote." Meg held her hand over each of the two finalists, but the crowd was evenly split. She moved back to the wild-haired contestant, who got a rousing response. She raised her hand behind the scantily clad wench and the crowd cheered. Then, the second contestant slid her peasant blouse farther down her shoulders, exposing cleavage created by her leather bustier. She raised her eyebrows, hinting that she might be willing to keep going.

Meg, standing behind the contestants, was oblivious to the provocative move, kept her hand over the woman's head. I jumped up, trying to get Meg's attention before there was a wardrobe malfunction, but Meg was focused on the crowd and their raucous response to the second wench.

Kerry was monitoring the crowd from the stage and realized the precarious position of the wench's top. He dashed from the shadows as the crowd egged the contestant on. She started to shrug, which threatened to release the minimal grip the elastic was providing on her upper arms. He stepped in front of her as the fabric started to slip. Meg caught on to the situation and together they hustled the wench into the wings. Kerry stood by while the contestant adjusted the neck of her blouse to a more modest position on her shoulders.

There were boos from a group of young men sitting in the beer garden, but the mother's with children were relieved. Meg rushed back onstage and awarded the prize to the crazy-haired wench, then escorted her to the back.

Meg returned after checking on Kerry and the other contestant, who were having a serious conversation in the wings.

"Please clear the street. We're going to have the first annual lutefisk toss. We have six contestants who've stepped forward to compete. Each will make one warm-up toss. Then, we'll let each of them make a throw that will be measured. The longest toss wins a $50 prize provided by the Dalbo Fish Company, the second largest lutefisk and pickled herring supplier in the United States." Meg paused and smiled, "Who knows, they may be the second largest in the world."

I stepped away, thinking I was done. Then Candy grabbed my arm. "We're the lutefisk throw judges too."

Candy followed me behind the bandshell, afraid of losing me in the gathering crowd. I hoped to catch Kerry before the lutefisk toss, hoping he'd found and arrested the murderer. He escorted the losing wench down the steps. She was unhappy, but Kerry had defused the situation and she walked away.

"Kerry! Do you have a second?"

Kerry looked haggard and tired but greeted me with a lopsided smile. "Hi, Peter. Who's your new friend?"

I introduced Candy and explained she was new to Two Harbors and had also been drafted to judge the talent contest and lutefisk throw.

Kerry shook her hand. "I'm relatively new in town too. But be warned, if you weren't born here, you'll always be an outsider."

215

"People have been very welcoming," Candy countered.

"That's Minnesota nice. There's a joke that a Minnesotan will give you directions anywhere, but his house. That's the real test of friendliness, if someone invites you over." Kerry put his hand on my shoulder. "Peter invited my family to his house and our sons are best friends. We've broken the ice."

I laughed. "But I'm not from here, either."

"Ah, but our wives are locals."

Candy looked away, sniffing. "What's that smell?"

We were behind the bandshell, near the Sons of Norway lutefisk serving area. "That's the lutefisk," I replied.

She wrinkled her nose. "It really stinks."

I smiled. "They decided to bake rather than boil it because it's less aromatic."

Candy grimaced. "This is the less smelly version?"

Kerry surveyed the line waiting for their serving of lutefisk and rutabaga. "There are a lot of people who like it. Look at the length of the line."

I saw a group of Whistling Pines residents walking across the park. Wendy was helping people off the van, now changed from her bathing suit into her wench costume.

I felt a tug on my hat. I turned and Kerry was batting at the ostrich plume. "Be careful

216

with your feather. It sticks out a long way behind the hat."

"Sorry, I'm unaccustomed to wearing an ostrich feather."

Candy laughed. "Your pirate outfit belongs in the front window of a costume shop."

"Or an antiques shop." Kerry batted at the feather again. "Be careful not to back up to a fire. Your feather could burst into flames."

Meg appeared next to us. "The sidewalk art contest is wrapping up on the east side of the park. Would you two go over and judge it?"

Candy's eyes lit up. "That sounds like fun!"

Kerry watched Meg hustle off to deal with another issue. "Meg's busier than a Minnesota nudist during mosquito season."

Candy snorted. "I should put that on plaques. The tourists would gobble them up at my store."

Kerry nodded. "I grant you the publishing rights."

We wound through the people in line for lutefisk and the treasure hunters to the parents and children lining the sidewalk on the east side of Owens park. The children's sidewalk art displayed a broad range of talent from stick figures to detailed multi-colored murals. We walked the length of the sidewalk, taking in the art and whispering our judgments as we walked.

A pirate t-shirt hugging a baby bump came into sight as we neared the end of the art. Jenny was watching Jeremy drawing Bart Simpson. He was focused and didn't see Candy and me approach.

"Jenny, this is Candy Mason who owns the cookware shop. Jenny is my wife and Jeremy, my son, is drawing Bart Simpson."

Jenny smiled, then watched Jeremy put the final touches on his artistic effort. "You can tell that's Bart Simpson?"

Candy laughed. "I think it's an abstract drawing of Bart."

Jenny looked down the sidewalk. "There are some talented kids."

"We got drafted as judges," Candy explained. "I think the lighthouse drawing is the best."

Jenny nodded. "Alice Pendleton is an art prodigy. She's a year older than Jeremy and the school has several pieces of her art on display in the hallways."

Candy looked at me as Meg walked up. "I think we have the winner."

Meg looked at Jeremy's rendering of Bart Simpson. "I think it's nearly a tie between Bart and the lighthouse, but I suppose the lighthouse is a little better."

Jeremy got up from his knees and stood back. "I think Bart is good." Then he looked at Alice's lighthouse. He drew a breath and cocked his head. "Alice always wins. She's really good."

Kerry steered me away from Jenny, Candy, and Jeremy, promising to return me in a minute. "The sheriff had some information about the Art West murder investigation."

"Is that why he wanted to talk in the alley?"

Kerry nodded as he led me to a quiet spot near a large tree. "He warned me off."

"What?"

"My call to the Ontario police about Colleen West's calls to a disposable phone apparently poked a hornet's nest. He told me any further investigation in that vein would jeopardize an ongoing international investigation."

"I don't know what that means. Are you supposed to drop a murder investigation?"

"He never said that."

"I'm confused," I said, taking off the bicorn hat.

"I got a call from the Bureau of Criminal Apprehension agent who processed the sailboat for evidence. Nearly all the fingerprints in the sailboat belonged to Collen or Art, except for one print they found under the counter where Art was repairing the broken wire. It didn't match anything in the National Automated Fingerprint Identification System (AFIS) database, so they thought it may have been left by one of the workers who built the boat.

"They would've left it at that, except they found traces of methamphetamine in the same recessed area under the counter. It appears the wiring problem may have been caused by someone jamming a package of meth under the counter."

My mind reeled as I processed the things Kerry told me. "So, the sheriff warns you off a murder investigation because of an ongoing international investigation. And the BCA says there were traces of meth, and an unknown fingerprint, in the recesses of West's sailboat. Do you think Art was removing meth smuggled from Canada when he was killed?"

"Colleen made the calls to Canada, and she was the sailor. I wonder if Art stumbled on the smuggled meth and was silenced."

"By whom? Colleen's accomplice?"

Kerry scanned the crowd. "The murder weapon was a muzzle-loading pistol. Have you noticed any Canadian pirates?"

"You mean a pirate who ends his sentences by asking, 'eh?'"

Kerry glared at me. "This is not a joke. Keep your eyes and ears open."

Candy broke away from Meg and searched the crowd for me. She waved and pointed toward the street where the lutefisk throwing competition was being arranged.

"I've got to run. It appears it's time to judge the lutefisk toss."

Kerry looked toward the street where tourists were gathering. "Just the sound of that makes me grimace. I don't see anything good resulting from men throwing hunks of lye-soaked cod."

I heard familiar female voices. They were angry and the volume was rising. Jenny rushed over. "Peter, you'd better step in. I'll take Jeremy to the face painter."

Olga Swanson and Hedvig Armstrong were Whistling Pines residents, and widowed sisters. They'd joined the line for lutefisk and were standing toe-to-toe. Olga had her finger in Hedvig's face. "You're a traitor! I'm going to tell the Sons of Norway to revoke your membership!"

Hedvig was equally incensed. "Just because I don't like lutefisk doesn't mean I'm not Norwegian!"

"Ha! You don't like pickled herring either. I can't believe we're related."

"Mother made us eat that stuff and I never liked them. I'm having potato sausage and lefse."

"It's Swedish!"

"What's Swedish?"

"The potato sausage is Swedish sausage. Real Norwegians don't eat Swedish sausage."

"I don't care what you call it. I like it."

Olga glared at her. "You must've been adopted from a Swedish family."

"That's low, Olga. If anyone's odd it's you. Everyone thinks you look more like Uncle Carl than Dad."

"I'm going to order two of those DNA tests. We'll find out who's adopted."

Hedvig stuck her nose into Olga's personal space. "Did you ever ask Mother why you have dark hair when all the rest of us are blondes? Did you?"

Olga turned red and was readying her comeback when Kerry pushed between them. "Let's cool off ladies."

"My sister started it!" Hedvig protested.

Kerry put up his hands. "And I ended it. The line is moving ahead. Move along or you'll lose your places."

Olga spun around and marched ahead, closing the gap between her and the person ahead. Kerry put his hand on Hedvig's arm. "Enjoy the sausage. You don't have to like lutefisk to be a real Norwegian."

Hedie nodded. "I know. Olga likes to argue."

Olga heard the conversation. "I don't like to argue! You're just wrong all the time!"

Kerry put up his hand, cutting off Hedvig's response. "Be the bigger person."

Hedvig nodded and leaned close to Kerry. "I like to yank her chain. It gives us something to talk about." She paused. "But that wisecrack about me being adopted, that hurt."

"You were adopted!" Olga said as she picked up a plate. She stepped up for her helping of lutefisk, served by a tall blond man in a white hat and apron.

"And you look more like Uncle Carl than Father!" Hedvig picked up her plate and held it to her chest, refusing the scoop of translucent lutefisk quivering on the serving spoon.

I directed Candy away from the Sons of Norway serving line. She looked over her shoulder. "You work at Whistling Pines. Is that the kind of thing you put up with?"

"Olga and Hedvig like to argue. Most of the residents are more reserved and happy."

"I saw the lutefisk. It really does look like gelatin."

I steered her toward the lutefisk throw contest area, in the street across from the bandshell. "Just wait until you see the competition. I think it'll be a hoot."

Chapter Ten

Candy and I joined the crowd now starting to clear the street and line the sidewalk. Long lines of people were strung down the sidewalk in front of the food trailers and the beer garden started to fill with people. I felt a hand on my elbow.

Kerry steered me toward the food trailers. "Can I borrow you for a couple minutes?"

The lutefisk toss wasn't taking shape and people were still milling in the street. "I guess so. What's up?"

"Jen Flanagan, the owner of the boat called 'Irish Heat' is working in the sausage tailer. This might be my best chance to talk to her."

I told Candy I'd be back in a couple minutes and followed Kerry to an aluminum trailer painted with sausages, menus, and prices. He knocked on the back door. A haggard woman wearing jeans and a sausage logo t-shirt and cap answered the door. She was surprised to see Kerry's uniform. "Um, I'm a little busy right now."

"We can talk here, right now or, we can go to the police station for this conversation."

Jen looked around to see if anyone was paying attention to us. "Okay, what's up?"

"Why have you been avoiding my calls?"

Jen nodded to the trailer. "I've been up to my eyeballs getting ready for today. It's not like we've had a lot of warning, so it's been a mad scramble to clean up the trailer, make sausages, smoke sausages, and get condiments. I was going to call you after we got through with buccaneer days."

"Tell me about Ashely Madison."

"I don't know anyone named Ashley."

Kerry paused, letting her know he was onto her. "The website, not the person."

Jen blushed and looked around furtively. "What about it?"

"You stopped responding to requests this week, about the same time Art West was killed on his sailboat. Were you at the marina Tuesday?"

"No. I told you I've been prepping for this festival all week. I haven't been anywhere near the marina."

"You quit responding to website requests before anyone knew about buccaneer days."

Jen nervously wiped her hands on a greasy rag. "I…uh…"

"Had Art West responded to your website post?"

"What? Art West? No!"

"Your absence from the website corresponds nicely with Art's death."

I could almost see Jen's façade crack. "I don't know what you mean."

"Why did you stop responding on the dating website. I know it has nothing to do with buccaneer days."

Jen stepped down from the trailer and got close to Kerry. "Listen, what I was doing was not illegal."

"No, but you probably wouldn't want me to ask Pat, your husband about it."

Jen drew a sharp breath. "Okay, here's the deal. I've been meeting men on the boat."

I leaned close. "You've been cheating."

Jen glared at me. "There's this fifty-mile rule about cheating on your spouse. You never cheat unless you're at least fifty miles from home. Well, I figured two miles of water was as good as fifty miles on land."

Kerry looked disgusted. "You've been cheating but keeping it two miles offshore. That doesn't explain why you quit earlier this week."

Jen wiped at non-existent grease on her hands and stared at the ground. "I had a little oops."

"Oops as in, you're pregnant?"

"Geez, no! Pat was one of the firemen who responded to the callout when Art's body was discovered. He went over to our boat, you know, just to check on things, after the ambulance left. He found a UPS package on the deck and opened it."

Kerry shook his head. "How incriminating was it?"

Jen bit her lip. "I'd ordered some lingerie, for an upcoming…sailboat tryst. Pat saw it for what it was and brought it home to confront me."

"So, now you're seeing a divorce lawyer?"

"It's not like that at all. I love Pat, I just wanted some variety and excitement."

Kerry shook his head. "Most people just go to a James Bond movie."

"Yeah, well I wanted a little more rush than that and it's hard to beat the rush of having an affair."

"What happened when Pat got home with your lingerie?"

"He was hot, but I convinced him I'd ordered it to surprise him. Our anniversary is coming up in a few weeks and I told him I'd planned on a romantic lake cruise."

"And he's bought that?" I asked.

Jen shrugged. "We're taking the boat out over our anniversary and I'm planning to wear the lingerie he found."

Kerry asked a few more questions, but it was clear that Jen Flanagan was guilty of nothing more than infidelity and hadn't been at the marina the day of the murder. We walked back to the crowd gathering for the lutefisk toss. "Like I've said, you've got to love a small town."

"You don't think that happens in the city, too?"

"I'm sure it does, but I'm willing to bet that all Flanagan's neighbors will know about Jen's affair, or some version of the truth, before they leave on their anniversary sail." Kerry stopped and put his hand on my arm. "I don't need to tell you that conversation with Jen goes no further. Right?"

I chuckled. "What conversation?"

"Thank you."

Candy was where I'd left her, now surrounded by people jostling for position along the edge of the street and eagerly anticipating the lutefisk toss. We approached Meg near a table topped with a plastic 5-gallon pail. The contestants were gathering nearby, a group of men, mostly in their twenties, and a young woman who looked vaguely familiar. Meg pushed through the crowd and pressed large pieces of yellow chalk into our hands.

"What are we supposed to do with these?"

"Go down the street and mark the spot where the lutefisk hits the pavement."

I looked at her. "Really. Won't we know where it hits?"

Meg shrugged. "Ole Lundquist suggested we mark the point of impact as the measurement spot rather than where the lutefisk comes to rest."

"Why?"

Ole, who looked about eighty, pushed between Meg and me. "Well," he started with a heavy Norwegian or Swedish accent (I can't tell the difference), there's two schools of thought on a lutefisk toss. One is to throw it as far as you can and let it just flop down where it hits. The other is to kind of bowl it down the street and use the rolling momentum to carry it a long way."

"And who wins?" I asked.

"We decided on the flop as the measure." He nodded at the young girl who was watching a man in a rubber apron and shoulder-length rubber gloves open the plastic pail. "Susan is the pitcher of the girls' fast-pitch softball team, and we think she's got an unfair advantage with her underhand delivery. That underhand pitching technique might get quite a roll down the street compared to the men who are going to throw overhand. We voted last night and decided to make the winning spot the place where the lutefisk first hits the street."

"That seems a little sexist," I said.

Ole shrugged. "It's not sexist. We just didn't want a girl to win." He turned and walked away.

I looked at Meg. "You're okay with this?"

Meg looked at Ole who was talking to the man struggling to open the lutefisk bucket. "They're the sponsors. They can set whatever rules they want, and since this is the first ever tournament, I don't know who'll have the advantage. The men are all former high school athletes. I think all of them are going to be able to throw it a long way. Speaking of which, why don't you and Candy go down the street about fifty yards and prepare to mark the landing spot."

"Is fifty yards the right distance?"

"I have no idea. We've never done this before." She smiled and leaned close. "That's part of why we decided to have the contestants take a warm-up throw, so we'd have some idea of how far it's going to fly."

Candy walked beside me, and we heard the pail pop as the pressure inside was released. I didn't want to think about what might've created the pressure, and certainly didn't want to entertain the thought that the Sons of Norway had neglected cold storage for the lutefisk. A gust of wind blew down the street and the smell of lutefisk caught up to us.

Candy's hand flew to her face. "Is that the lutefisk I smell?"

"Yup."

She grabbed my arm. "We won't get any on our clothes, will we?"

"I doubt it, but the smell might permeate our clothes and skin even if we don't get hit."

"Really?"

"I'm not a lutefisk expert but remember what the woman said about her parents' house smelling like lutefisk until New Year's Day."

"Geez. I had no idea what I was getting into when Meg asked if I'd volunteer to be a judge."

We got to our appointed spot and I looked toward where a man wearing long rubber gloves and a plastic apron was laying hunks of white lutefisk on the table. "At least you volunteered. I was drafted."

"How you got drafted into this?"

"I'm the recreation director at Whistling Pines, the senior residence. My boss asked me to go to the chamber of commerce organizing meeting."

"Oh, I've heard about your wedding. I guess it was quite a show." Candy paused in thought. "Didn't you and your wife move into the haunted house, too?"

"That's me."

Candy, who was about my age, giggled. "I heard about the ghost chase in your living room. I ate breakfast at Judy's the morning after the band delivered your Christmas tree. I nearly spit my coffee."

"It's much funnier now than it was at the time."

After being handed a megaphone by the fire chief, Ole announced the Sons of Norway sponsorship and invited any interested Scandinavians to join the Sons for coffee and pie on the third Thursday evening of any month. He then explained the competition rules. Each contestant got one practice throw, overhand or underhand, and the first point of impact was the official measurement spot.

A tall, lanky blond guy stepped forward and chose a piece of lutefisk from the table. He cocked his arm like a quarterback and stepped into the throw, using his full body to provide propulsion. The crowd was silent as he followed through, opened his fingers, and the lutefisk oozed out, splattering his face on the follow through. The biggest piece making forward progress was the size of a golf ball and it landed about five feet in front of the table. The crowd roared as the contestant swore and tried to shake the stinky, snotty mess from his hand. A woman rushed forward with a roll of paper towels and helped him wipe his hands and face clean.

Ole raised the megaphone and clucked his tongue. "Well, I guess maybe the football throw ain't the best strategy. Let's have contestant number two."

A heavier man, who looked like a lumberjack, prodded a few pieces of lutefisk with his finger before choosing a hunk. He took a pose like a baseball pitcher, stepped into the throw, and using a two-finger grip, split the lump of lutefisk in half, each piece falling at his feet.

The crowd howled and the pitcher turned red, refusing the paper towels and shaking his pitching hand to get the oozing mess off them.

Ole introduced the contestants one-by-one, each having about the same result. The female fast-pitch contestant, learning from the others, opted for a slow, underhand lob. The lutefisk arced high into the air, flying twenty yards before it splatted on the street. She got cheers from the crowd and took a bow.

The last contestant was stocky, like a sumo wrestler. He pulled on a pair of dishwashing gloves before selecting his piece of lutefisk. The crowd watched with curiosity as he stepped back from the table and cradled the lump of fish next to his ear with his right hand, he then extended his left arm. He took a step, then used a shotput move to launch his lutefisk. His lump stayed intact and landed twice as far down the street as anyone else's toss. The crowd cheered and he nodded his appreciation to them.

Ole announced that as the end of the warm-up and suggested anyone who needed a refreshment should get it now, before the start of the measured competition. Candy looked worried.

"What's the matter?"

"Who's going to clean up this mess? I saw a stray cat sniff the lutefisk and walk away."

"That's why the firemen are here. They're going to hose down the street after the contest is over."

She nodded, then cocked her head, looking past me. She pointed toward the lake. "Are there naked people on that boat?"

The naturist cruise was well offshore, but the exposed white skin stood out in the sunlight. "I'm sure they're wearing bathing suits."

"My eyesight is pretty good. I don't think they are."

I was at a loss for words. "I think Ole's ready to announce the competition." I held up my chalk, ready to dash out and mark the landing spot.

The competitors learned from the shotput approach, and most chose an underhand toss. No one had a repeat of the glob disintegrating in hand, but the longest toss of the first four was twenty yards. Candy and I dashed into the street after each throw to mark the landing spot, not that any of the snotty globs went more than an inch or two after it hit the pavement.

The young woman selected her piece and used a little more oomph than her first throw, landing her throw ahead of the shotput practice throw. The crowd cheered.

The next throws fell well short and the last competitor pulled on his rubber gloves, choosing from the last ten pieces of fish. He poked all of them with his finger, apparently looking for a firmer piece. He took the shotput pose, danced forward, and the lutefisk arched through the air. I moved near where I expected it to land and reached out with my chalk as soon as it hit.

I looked at the mark, then up at Candy. "I think it's a tie."

She squatted down, then nodded. "Yes."

I stood up and yelled to Ole. "It's a tie!"

Ole looked confused. "A tie?" He yelled over the megaphone.

"Yes. They're dead even!"

Ole frowned, not pleased that "the girl" was still in it. "Well then, I guess we need a tie-breaker throw from the two leading contestants."

He waved the pitcher to the table and she picked a piece of lutefisk, hefted it a bit, then stepped into her underhand throw. A group of young women crowded the roadway, cheering. Each had a plastic beer cup and wore softball uniforms matching the pitcher. They were uninhibited in their support of their teammate. With two practice throws of experience, she did a slow windup, then lofted a toss that went a full five feet past her best previous attempt. Her teammates went wild, cheering and sloshing beer.

With a satisfied smile, the pitcher stepped back and bowed to the crowd.

Ole looked around for the final contestant but didn't see him. "Hey, somebody get Shawn back over here. He's got to throw again."

235

Shawn emerged from the crowd and walked up to the table. He whispered to Ole, who looked around the table and under the feet of the people now crowding the area. He finally picked up the megaphone. "Shawn's misplaced his gloves. If someone has his rubber gloves, please bring them to the table."

The women's softball team talked among themselves, then started to chant, "Make him throw. Make him throw."

A murmur went through the crowd, but no one stepped forward with Shawn's rubber gloves. A voice from the beer garden shouted, "A real man doesn't need gloves to touch a hunk of fish!"

Shawn turned red and faced the direction the voice had come from. "Oh yeah, come over here and say that to my face!"

"I don't want to get any closer than this to your ugly mug!"

Kerry pushed through the crowd and stepped next to Candy and me. "I don't like where this is heading."

Shawn picked up a piece of lutefisk and hurled it toward the voice. Having thrown, rather than tossing the lump, it broke into pieces and splattered a number of bystanders who shouted and swore. One of them dashed into the street and picked up one of the pieces that had tied the match and hurled it at Shawn.

His aim was poor, and like the losing throws, the lutefisk broke into pieces, showering another part of the crowd.

Kerry stepped forward with his hands in the air, shouting for order. No one heard him and one of the few people who noticed him stepped into the street, grabbed the other remaining lump of lutefisk, and tossed it at Kerry.

He was quick and saw the glob flying at him, unlike Candy and I who were shielded from view by Kerry. He ducked, and the fragmented, snotty, stinky glob hit Candy and me in our faces.

Kerry grabbed the guy who'd thrown the lump at him and pulled his arm behind his back.

I wiped my face, then realized Candy was staring at me in shock with slime dripping off her chin. "Peter, I think I got some in my eyes. Will I go blind?"

I led her to the park where the fire department had a first aid station. The EMT assured Candy she wouldn't suffer permanent eye damage and helped flush her eyes and wipe the stinking ooze off her face and shirt.

A melee was going on in the street, with people throwing smaller and smaller pieces of lutefisk at each other. That lasted only a few moments until there weren't any big enough pieces left to throw, the crowd then meandering to the park, laughing and wiping bits of white slimy fish from their faces and clothing.

"Please clear the street," Ole announced via megaphone as the firemen opened a hose and washed the slimy mess down the storm sewer drains.

Kerry emerged from the crowd and walked up to Candy and me, looking sheepish. "Sorry. I ducked out of reflex."

I waved off his apology. "It'll come out in the wash, I'm sure."

Candy looked at me. "Really, you think this stink will go away in the laundry?"

I shrugged. "Maybe if you soak your clothes in tomato juice first, like after you get sprayed by a skunk."

Kerry was struggling to stifle his laughter. "I heard buttermilk soaks work pretty well too."

I saw the Whistling Pines van moving from its parking spot. The tour boat was docked and the bikini-clad first mate was helping people across the gangway. The people were smiling and shaking hands like they'd all made friends. Alma's mink coat was tastefully closed and even Hulda Packer was smiling. Wendy stepped out of the van and aided the residents up the steps. A line had formed near the gangway and it appeared the afternoon cruise had also sold out.

Chapter Eleven

Meg Cochran rushed up, stopping short when she saw and smelled the lutefisk on my coat and shirt. "Where are the rest of the judges?"

Having been preoccupied with my own plight during the lutefisk fight, I'd lost track of everyone but Candy, who'd been alongside me the entire time. I looked around and saw lots of tourists, but none of the other judges. "I don't know where they went."

"They all ran for cover when the lutefisk started flying," Kerry explained.

Meg sighed and shook her head. "I need a couple people to ride out with the regatta officials. You two are the only ones I can find."

I put up my hand. "I think Candy and I have contributed enough. I'm going home to shower and change."

Meg was a force of nature. "You're already slimy and stinky. Why not go out on the boats with the regatta officials?" Meg pinched her nose. "And no one in the crowd wants to be around you."

"I'd really like to go home and shower." Candy nodded her agreement.

Kerry was about to put his arm over my shoulder when he noted some slime on my coat. He reconsidered and patted my bicep.

240

"Let's be realistic. You don't want to sit in your car until you've aired out a while, or at least until the slime dries. The stink will get into your car seat and will be there for months."

Two men wearing life jackets walked up from the historical society building. "Meg, have you found crewmembers for us?"

She nodded. "Candy and Peter are the only judges I can locate."

The taller man, Kurt, whom I recognized from wine tastings at the liquor store, nodded to me. "Peter pirate, why don't you come with me. Your wench can ride with Greg."

Greg Oien was a Navy vet I recognized from the VFW. He nodded to Candy. "Come with me. I'll let Kurt have the sailor; he needs all the help he can get."

I reluctantly fell in step with Kurt. "What did Greg mean?"

"I grew up living on White Bear Lake, and until two years ago all my boating experience was there. Greg kids me that I grew up sailing on a pond while he was on the ocean."

I looked at Kurt skeptically. "And I'm supposed to be a big help for you?"

"Greg said you'd been in the Navy."

"I was a corpsman attached to a Marine unit in Iraq. The only time I've been on a ship is when the Marines spent two weeks in a landing ship on the Black Sea."

Kurt shook his head as we reached his boat. "Do you know how to untie a line?"

"That much I can handle."

"Untie the aft line."

I walked to the back of the boat and loosed the aft rope, then carefully wound it around my arm before hopping onto the Boston Whaler fishing boat.

Kurt smiled as I set the coiled rope neatly on the rear deck. "You're way ahead of Candy." He pointed to Greg and Candy. She was getting a lesson on fore and aft, then on handling the lines."

Kurt's twin outboard motors rumbled to life and we eased away from the quay. He handed me a life jacket that I secured over my pirate coat. Greg and Candy were still dealing with his lines when Kurt turned the boat toward the lake.

"What are we doing?"

"We're the regatta officials, and I've got a GPS location where we're supposed to be stationed. The sailboats have to turn around us before circling back to make a turn at Greg's boat. Then they race back to the yacht club boat at the marina."

"So, our role is to stay in one spot and make sure all the boats go around us?"

Kurt nodded, then grimaced as he turned into the wind. "I don't mean to be nasty, but I'd like you to stay downwind."

I realized the wind was blowing from me toward Kurt. "I'll move starboard."

"What did you get into? It smells like you got dipped in rotten fish and dragged through a swamp."

"Candy and I were judging the Sons of Norway lutefisk toss when it devolved into a food fight. We took a direct hit."

"I overheard someone saying the lutefisk for the competition got left out overnight when they got busy cooking up the rest of the meal." He paused. "Do you think lutefisk spoils? I mean, it's dried cod soaked in lye. Can it go bad?"

I closed my eyes. "I'm sure leaving a pail of it in the sun for a day isn't going to improve it."

Kurt kept his eyes on a GPS monitor as he slowed the boat. "I have a friend who's a big catfish aficionado. He buys chicken livers, puts hooks into them, then leaves them in a pail of blood in the sunshine for a day. He says that's the best catfish bait he's ever used."

"Catfish like them?"

Kurt chuckled. "Charlie says he thinks they bite it just to get the stink out of the river."

"You should suggest lutefisk as an alternate to chicken livers."

With the motors idling, the wind pushed us around. Kurt glared at me, wrinkling his nose. "You're upwind again."

"Sorry," I said, moving to the port side of the boat.

243

As sails became visible on the horizon, Kurt took out a pair of binoculars. "There's not a lot of wind today, that'll favor the more experienced sailors."

"What do you mean?"

Kurt continued looking through the binoculars. "It's more difficult to arrange your sails and tack when the winds are mild. Anyone can throw up a spinnaker and race with the wind, but it takes more savvy to make the most of mild winds. I think we'll see the field pretty well spread out this afternoon."

The sails looked larger as they approached, going from tiny triangles on the horizon to large white sails billowing in the wind. "There's a square sail in the back," I said.

Kurt snorted. "That's the Sons of Norway Viking ship. Their sail is yellow and blue, the colors of the Swedish flag."

"They're bringing up the rear."

Kurt put down the binoculars and looked at me. "They'll catch up."

"Their sail is better?"

"They're not in the race. They're just along to annoy the real sailors. I'm sure they've got their motor running."

As the lead boats approached within a quarter mile, I saw that the Viking ship had overtaken the lagging sailboats. A puff of white smoke exploded out of the Viking ship. A few seconds later, I heard a boom.

Kurt looked at me, shaking his head. "The Vikings are attacking."

"What?"

"The Sons of Norway found a small cannon and they're firing at the sailboats as they pass."

"Is that legal?"

Kurt snorted. "I don't know that it's illegal, but it's not a normal part of a regatta."

The two lead boats were side-by-side as they neared us, close enough for me to see the captain and crews. They looked intense as they passed.

"Watch the turn," Kurt said. "The turns might decide the race."

The boats flew past us, keeled away, their sails filled with wind. First one boat, then the other, turned sharply. The sails snapped as the boom swung from starboard to port. The crew ducked under the passing boom and moved to the opposite side of the boat. Within seconds they'd changed directions and were around us, on their way toward Greg and Candy.

"That was impressive," I said, watching the leaders sail away from us."

"Mark and Dave are good sailors. They're always among the top three finishers."

I looked at a group of four boats approaching with the Viking ship among them. "Which one of these is the other who finishes in the top three?"

Kurt shook his head. "We lost that captain. He was the guy shot on his boat."

I pictured the dead man in the cabin of his boat, a hole in his chest and blood pooled on the deck around him. "Art West?"

Kurt nodded. "Colleen and Art were always first or second. It's a shame Art's gone, West's sailboat was like the rabbit the other greyhounds chased."

I looked at the retreating sails, noting a logo on one. "What's the marking on that sail?"

"Dave Carlson has a corporate sponsor. He got a sail from them with the company logo. I guess if you're good enough, the sponsors will fly you around the world to compete."

"There's money in amateur sailboat racing?"

Kurt shrugged. "I guess there is if you're winning and marketing yourself."

The next group of boats was nearly abreast of us when the Viking ship fired another cannon volley. Crew members on the boat closest to them brought out a hose and squirted it at the Vikings.

The sailboats passed us and started their turn. The Viking ship turned before it got to us, exposing the profile. The Sons of Norway had cut a plywood dragon's head and affixed it to the bow of their boat, along with colorful round plywood shields. I heard the rumble of their motor as they went past.

By turning before getting to us, they were now ahead of the group.

The Vikings fired one more cannon volley at the sailboats, then raced off to catch the leaders.

Kurt shook his head. "The leaders are serious about winning the race. They won't be pleased about the Vikings harassing them."

We stayed in position until the last straggler turned around us. Then Kurt fired up the outboards and we motored wide of the sailboats and headed toward the harbor.

"You can drop me off by the historical society gift shop."

Kurt was focused on the sailboats ahead of us and wasn't even complaining about me being upwind. "I think we need to get to the finish line. The leaders aren't going to find humor in the Sons of Norway harassment."

With the outboards at full throttle, we quickly caught up and passed the middle group of sailboats. The Viking ship and the leaders were still well ahead of us, with the Viking ship quickly closing the gap.

Smoke billowed from the Vikings as they neared the leaders. One of the Viking sailors was on the bow. He wore a helmet with horns and was shaking a sword at the two leading boats.

The Viking ship was maneuvering itself to go between the leaders when I saw one of the crew members of the leading sailboat throw something overboard. I couldn't see what he'd thrown, but the Viking captain veered hard port to miss whatever it was. Within seconds the Vikings slowed. and the leaders pulled away.

"What happened?" I asked.

"One of the leading boats threw a coil of line overboard and it's fouled the Viking's propeller."

"That seems cruel."

Kurt slowed the motors and eased alongside the Vikings. "It's more than cruel. It might've burned up a motor that'll cost a thousand dollars or more to repair."

Kurt leaned on the railing. "Toss me a line and we'll tow you into the harbor."

A rope coiled through the air and flopped across the stern of Kurt's boat. He tied it off and eased ahead, pulling out the slack before adding more power.

"We should call the police chief," I said as we motored along.

Kurt looked at me and shook his head. "It's up to the boat captains. They can lodge a complaint with the yacht club and might even notify the Coast Guard. I doubt that will happen because the Vikings were too close and shouldn't have been harassing the legitimate sailors. I imagine a number of them will be talking to the yacht club and the owner of the Viking ship will be in jeopardy of losing his membership."

"But they burned up an expensive motor!"

Kurt shrugged. "That may be the cost of being a pirate."

Unable to find anyone to drive stinky judges to town, Candy and I were stuck at the Knife River Marina as the sailboats returned and tied up. I found a vending machine in the marina office and bought Candy and myself cans of soda pop before the harbormaster complained about our smell and sent us out to the docks.

Candy sniffed the air. "I can hardly smell the lutefisk over the other harbor smells."

I was amazed that my nose hadn't tired of the smell, but the reality was we were still much stinkier than the smelliest fishing boat in the commercial fleet. "I don't think even soaking our clothes in diesel oil would cover the smell."

Kurt was helping the Sons of Norway get their boat into a slip as the sailboats came into the harbor. I watched the winning boat tie up in their slip as a fishing charter boat followed the trailing sailboats into the marina. The second-place sailboat immediately lowered an inflatable dinghy that raced across the marina toward the Viking ship.

I handed my can of soda to Candy. "Hang onto this."

"What's going on?"

"I think the sailboat owner is going to express his extreme displeasure with the Norwegians." I trotted down the dock to the Viking ship, arriving just as the dinghy tied off.

The dinghy's captain, dressed in a pirate outfit complete with saber and pistol, jumped onto the dock and stalked toward the Vikings, who were leaning over the dock, inspecting the damage to their motor. The Vikings were distracted, on their hands and knees, looking at the keel of their boat.

Dave Carlson, dressed as a pirate stomped up, expecting a reaction from the Vikings. When none of the Vikings noticed him, he stepped behind the biggest Norwegian, planted his boot on the man's butt, and pushed. The Viking sprawled into the water. Before the others realized what had happened, Dave pushed two more Vikings into the cold harbor.

"Hey, cut that out!" A younger Viking got up before the pirate reached him. "What'cha think you're doing?" he asked, his fists clenched.

"You damned Norwegians nearly ruined the race!"

"What?"

"We were racing and you interfered.

"It's a festival, Dave, you're taking it too seriously."

The pirate seethed and I stepped between the two men while Kurt, Greg and

250

the other Vikings pulled their comrades out of the water. "Easy," I said. "There's no need to get physical." Dave clenched and unclenched his fists, then felt the sword. He was reaching for the hilt when I put my hands up. "Dave, talk to the harbormaster or the yacht club if you want to lodge a complaint. We're done here."

Dave was now confronted by seven of us and saw the wisdom in my suggestion. He raised his hand and pointed it at me. "THIS. IS. NOT. OVER." He walked up to me and got into my personal space. "You're that guy who was here with the police chief the other day. Peter, right. Peter Rogers."

I took a step back. "I'm one of the judges, not a party to anything that happened."

"You should've stopped those air-headed Norwegians." He stalked away, going toward the marina office.

Greg Oien appeared next to me and we watched him leave. "He's a hothead, that one. You might come back to your boat and find it sunk with the seacocks open."

"I don't own a boat."

Greg smiled. "That's probably for the best." Then he sniffed the air and took a step back. "I suppose you need a ride back to town."

"Yeah, both Candy and I need a ride."

"You ever ride in the back of a pickup?"

"Not in a while."

Greg nodded and sniffed again. "I think that's your only option."

A green pickup with red and blue lights pulsing in its grille sped into the parking lot and slid to a stop. Two officers in bulletproof vests walked to the marina office. I pulled out my phone and dialed Kerry's number.

"What's up, Peter?"

"Two game wardens just pulled into the marina parking lot with their flashers on. You might want to get down here to back them up."

"They usually call the county sheriff's department if they need assistance."

"Something's going on. A boat with flashers just pulled past the jetty and is blocking the marina entrance."

"Hang on, I'm getting chatter on the radio." As I waited, I looked around the marina and noticed frantic activity on the fishing charter that arrived with the sailboats. "The department of natural resources just requested backup from any available officer at the marina. I'm on my way."

The two DNR officers ran out of the marina office with Ray, the harbormaster, pointing toward the fishing charter that had just docked. I shut down my phone and watched seagulls swarming around the charter boat as the crew repeatedly threw things into the water.

Candy was very concerned. "What do you suppose is going on?"

"Let's walk over."

We walked the lanes of dock until we were approaching the fishing boat. One DNR officer was talking to the crew while a second man wielded a long-handled landing net off the transom of the boat. As we neared, I could see him pulling large, dead fish out of the water and flipping them onto the boat.

We stopped twenty feet behind the boat and watched. The charter captain was arguing with the DNR officer while his mate stood silently by.

"What kind of fish are those?" Candy asked as two large silver fish were flipped from the marina waters onto the boat deck.

"I'm not a fisherman, but they look like some kind of salmon or lake trout."

"That cop has pulled out like fifteen fish. What's the limit?"

"Based on the reaction of the game wardens, I'd guess it's fewer than the number on their deck."

The second DNR officer ended his netting and walked to the captain as the boat with flashing lights approached the stern of the fishing boat. A man and a woman in Coast Guard uniforms tied off their boat and joined the group on the fishing boat.

Candy looked at me. "Is that the Navy?"

"They're probably Coast Guard."

"Why would they be here with the game wardens?"

I heard the wail of a siren approaching and seconds later an unmarked car sped into the parking lot and parked next to the DNR pickup.

Kerry jogged onto the dock and stopped next to us. "What's going on?"

"The crew was throwing fish into the water and the DNR was fishing them back out with a landing net. I'm not sure what the Coast Guard is doing, but they showed up about the same time as the DNR."

A Minnesota State Patrol trooper pulled into the parking lot showing less urgency than the DNR officers or Kerry. He carefully placed a maroon Smokey the Bear hat on his head and walked down the dock.

He stopped next to Kerry and watched the activity on the boat. "Looks like the fish cops and Coasties have this under control."

Kerry nodded. "Unless someone pulls out a gun, we're probably not needed." He paused. "Do you know what's going on?"

"The DNR has had Captain Casey under surveillance for the entire summer. They suspect him of taking over his limit on the days he doesn't have bookings so he can provide full limits of fish to all his charter patrons."

Candy looked at him. "Is that legal?"

The trooper laughed. "No. That would be why they're having this discussion with him."

One of the DNR officers took the crewman aside and escorted him onto the dock. They walked far enough away from the boat to be out of our hearing and away from Captain Casey who was nearly frothing at the mouth.

"The captain seems very agitated," Candy observed.

The trooper nodded. "I suspect officer Collins just explained the laws pertaining to overharvesting lake trout. They can seize his boat and all his fishing gear, then auction it off."

Candy's eyes went wide. "They can take his boat for catching too many fish?"

The trooper nodded. "Over the course of the investigation, they have watched him catch more than two hundred fish over his limit. The judges really throw the book at people who do that. They take an even dimmer view of charter captains who do things like that, because they're expected to be stewards of the fishery and model the behavior expected of all sportfishermen."

I looked at Kerry. "That's why Captain Casey didn't want to admit he was on the dock when Art West was shot. He and his mate were carrying a cooler full of illegal fish. If he told you he'd heard the shot, he might have to explain what he and his mate were doing."

The trooper looked at Kerry and smiled. "The DNR isn't happy with you. They've been running this operation for two months and because you stuck your nose into it, they had to wrap it up and make the arrests now."

Kerry shrugged. "If they'd told me what they were up to I would've quietly stood aside. No one told me they had an overlapping investigation. That left me calling people they didn't want spoken with and suspicious about Captain Casey's evasion on the day Art West was killed."

The trooper smiled and nodded toward Captain Casey, who was now being restrained by the Coast Guard officers after getting in the DNR officer's face and letting loose with a stream of profanity that would make a mule skinner blush. "This will piss off the DNR even more, but I bet the captain would be happy to have a heart-to-heart talk with you, in great detail, if you make an arrangement with the county attorney that would allow him to keep his boat in return for his cooperation."

Kerry smiled and pulled out his phone. "That's an inspired suggestion." Kerry dialed a number as he walked away from us.

Candy looked at the trooper. "Won't the game wardens get mad at the chief for doing that?"

The trooper looked at Kerry, then at the captain. "I think they'll be way past mad if the chief can work out a plea bargain before they even get the captain to the county jail."

Candy seemed confused. "Don't you guys all work together?"

The trooper nodded. "Most of the time." He turned. "I don't think they need me."

Candy watched the trooper walk away. "I'm very confused."

"A murder investigation trumps an arrest over a wildlife violation. It's going to irritate the DNR officers to no end if Kerry can get the county attorney to give Captain Casey partial immunity in return for information that will break open the Art West murder investigation. The key will be whether the captain can provide enough information about the murder investigation to make it worthwhile to give him leniency on the fish violation."

Greg Oien had been patiently waiting by his pickup, texting and answering voicemails. He walked out to us. "Are you guys ready to go back to town?

"Yes, we're through here."

We walked the dock back toward the marina store with Greg. "When was the last time you guys rode in the back of a pickup?"

Candy looked at me, then at Greg. "I haven't ever ridden in a pickup bed."

Greg burst into a smile. "This is your lucky day!"

"C'mon, Greg. You're not going to make us ride in the back of the pickup," I pled.

"You're not riding in the front reeking of lutefisk. Uh uh."

Greg helped us into the pickup bed. Candy sat next to the tailgate and I leaned against the back of the cab. "You must be a city kid," I said.

"Why?"

"Country kids know sitting next to the tailgate gets you bounced around the most. The back end bounces twice as much as the back wheels, which sometimes leaves you airborne."

Candy moved beside me behind the cab. "What other city kid things should I avoid?"

"Two Harbors is a small town. Never criticize anyone in a public place, you might be standing next to their best friend or cousin."

"Really?"

"I overheard a guy in Judy's café say that his daughter had a fight with the garbage hauler's wife's best friend. The garbage truck wouldn't pick up his garbage can if it weighed over twenty pounds and wouldn't take more than one can or bag from their house. He gave up after a few months and hauled his garbage to the landfill in his pickup."

Candy sighed. "As a shop owner, I learned that one long ago. I can't afford to alienate customers."

Greg backed up, then turned and eased through the parking lot.

Candy looked concerned. "Peter, are you afraid of that guy's threat?"

"He was blowing off steam. Once he cools down things will be okay."

Candy obviously didn't believe me and was rattled by the exchange. I usually react to situations like that by becoming quiet and reflective. Candy was an extrovert who processed her feelings out loud. "I was really freaked. I mean, he was so mad, seething. I thought he was going to draw his sword and start slashing people."

"I was sure that wasn't going to happen. People have a filter that kicks in before they actually start throwing punches or stabbing others."

"That happens in bars."

Greg pulled onto the highway and I had to nearly yell to be heard over the rushing wind. "It's different when liquor or drugs are involved. They lower people's inhibitions.

Candy glanced at me and frowned. "You know a lot of stuff. Are you a cop?"

"No, just a guy who's knocked around a bit."

She was still full of nervous energy, so Candy told me her life story, starting with growing up in St. Cloud, in central Minnesota, attending the university there, while working as a waitress in a pizza place. She continued as I watched a dark-colored SUV approach us from behind. Greg might've been going a bit under the speed limit to minimize the discomfort of our ride, but the SUV was approaching fast.

Trying to discern the driver's face, I studied the windshield as he approached. About the time I saw the shape of his face, he pulled up a red bandana, leaving only his eyes and dark hair visible. "Shit," I said, interrupting Candy's life story.

"What?"

"The guy in the SUV just covered his face."

Candy looked stricken as she turned to watch the rapidly approaching SUV. In seconds it was on Greg's bumper. I tapped the glass of the back window to warn Greg. That was exactly the wrong thing to do because he looked over his shoulder at me just as the SUV, it's windows darkened, swerved to pass.

Pointing ahead, I tried to make Greg understand what was happening. He looked at me, then turned his head back just as the SUV cut him off. Greg twisted the wheel to avoid hitting the SUV, throwing Candy and me against the side of the pickup box. The pickup flew over the gravel shoulder of the road and into the ditch. To Greg's credit, he kept the vehicle under control, braking and steering down the water-filled ditch without rolling the pickup or crashing into the trees lining the far side of the ditch.

He found a dry area as he slowed and eased the truck onto the shoulder. Then he stopped and jumped out of the cab. "Are you guys okay?"

I blew out a breath and pushed myself up from the pickup bed. "I'll have some bruises, but nothing's broken."

Candy groped around and found her glasses. They were slightly askew. "I'm okay. I got thrown into Peter when you swerved, and he took the brunt of the punishment."

Greg turned and looked down the empty road. "He didn't even stop to apologize."

"He did it on purpose."

Greg looked disgusted. "Some stupid, thrill-seeking kid driving daddy's truck, I suppose."

"Or a vindictive pirate."

Greg frowned. "Do you think that was the idiot from the dock?"

"He tried to hide his face, but I'm pretty sure it was Dave."

A car stopped behind us to see if we needed assistance. While Greg assured them we were okay, I called the police chief on my cellphone and explained what had happened.

"Did you get his license number?"

"Kerry, I was trying to keep from getting thrown out of the pickup bed. I wasn't really focused on collecting evidence."

"Was he close enough to identify?"

"He pulled a bandana over his face. I think it was Dave, the angry pirate."

There was a pause. "So, this was definitely not an accident."

"It wasn't an accident. Have your folks keep an eye out for a black SUV with the rear windows darkened. There can't be too many of those around town."

"I'll mention it to them, but everyone's preoccupied after the fight broke out in the beer garden. A few guys were over served and expressed their displeasure when refused more beer."

Greg had been listening to my half of the conversation and raised his eyebrows, hopeful the police would find the driver. I shook my head and ended the call. "The cops are busy dealing with drunken pirates. They may get time to look for the SUV later."

Greg nodded to the pickup bed. "Hop in. I'll get you into town."

Candy hesitated. "Can't we ride inside the truck?"

Standing downwind from us, Greg sniffed the air. "I don't think so. If anything, you're gamier than before. I think the lutefisk slime is starting to ferment on you."

Candy sat next to me in the pickup bed and adjusted her bent glasses. "Does lutefisk really ferment?"

"Before today, I would've said no. I thought the lye soak would make it impervious to bacteria." I sniffed the air rushing around us. "But setting the pail of lutefisk in the sun for a day before the contest seems to have brought it to a new level of…reekiness."

Candy snorted. "Is reekiness even a word?"

I shrugged. "Don't you think it fits?"

"I'll put reekiness on my Facebook page and see what comments I get."

Back in town, I thanked Greg and said goodbye to Candy. I paused at my car, trying to decide how to minimize the stink carried in by my clothing. I got a plastic garbage bag from the Sons of Norway, who were shutting down their lutefisk and potato sausage concession. I declined an offer to buy discounted leftover lutefisk and pickled herring and walked back to my car. I put my coat, shirt, shoes, and socks into the bag, tied it, and stowed it in the trunk.

With the car windows open and the vent blasting, I could hardly smell the lutefisk. On arriving home, I retrieved the garbage bag from the trunk and brought it in the house, turning immediately down the basement stairs. I threw the coat and pants, which I'm sure were supposed to be dry cleaned, into the wash with the shirt and socks. I set the shoes next to the floor drain, poured water over them, then stuck a dryer sheet inside each.

Halfway up the stairs I heard Jenny gagging. I froze, waiting to see what would happen, but sure of the cause. After a few seconds, I heard conversation and the basement door opened a crack.

"Dad, is that you?"

"Yeah. I just threw a load of clothes in the washer."

"Mom says that if it's you that smells, you should hose yourself off in the backyard before you come back in the house."

Resigned to standing in the yard in my underwear, I trudged up the stairs. "I'll be out back. See if we have any tomato juice."

Jeremy sniffed as I passed. "What's that stink?"

"Lutefisk."

"What's that?"

"It's a traditional Scandinavian Christmas food made from cod."

Jenny yelled from somewhere upstairs. "I can still smell you. Go outside!"

I grabbed the bottle of dish soap off the counter and lathered repeatedly, using the hose to rinse myself. After four repeats I was out of dish soap and it seemed like the lemony fresh scent had overpowered the fishy lutefisk smell. Having forgotten a towel in my rush to get outside, I stepped into the kitchen dripping water on the floor.

Jeremy had been watching out the kitchen window. He stood on a chair and stared at me. "You look like Larsons' dog after they wash him."

"Please get a bath towel for me."

Jeremy hopped down and walked upstairs, in no apparent rush. I heard voices upstairs and Jeremy returned without a towel. "Mom says she doesn't want that stink on any of her good towels. She said you should dry off with paper towels, then burn them."

I took a handful of paper towels and rubbed my hair. The dish soap was not meant to replace shampoo and my hair felt like straw as it dried. Jeremy watched, fascinated.

"Did you find any tomato juice?" I asked.

He shook his head. "There's grape juice if you're thirsty. Or, I could open a beer for you."

"Tomato juice cuts the smell when you get sprayed by a skunk."

"You said…"

"Yes, it was lutefisk smell. I thought the tomato juice might work on that smell too."

Jeremy sniffed the air. "You don't smell as bad as you did."

"I'm not sure that's good enough for your mom."

Footsteps proceeded down the steps and Jenny stepped into the doorway, holding her nose. "What did you get into?"

"There was fiasco at the lutefisk throw. I got caught in the crossfire."

"I've had lutefisk and it doesn't smell that bad."

"Someone left the bucket in the sun for a day and it got a little extra smelly." Jenny let go of her nose, sniffed the air, then ran for the upstairs bathroom. I looked at Jeremy. "I just failed the smell test."

He sniffed the air again. "It's a lot better, but it's still there."

I remembered a remedy a veterinarian had suggested to one of his clients. "Get the brown bottle of hydrogen peroxide out of the medicine cabinet." I got a pail from under the sink and poured a tablespoon of the backup dish soap into it, with a gallon of water.

Jeremy bounced into the kitchen with the brown peroxide bottle and handed it to me. "What's that for?"

I poured the entire pint of peroxide in the bucket, mixed it up, and grabbed a sponge. "This is supposed to kill skunk smell."

I was swabbing myself with the peroxide solution when I noticed our neighbor, Mrs. Piper watching me from her back porch. Wearing only my underwear, I waved and she ducked back inside the house. After two scrubs that used up all the peroxide mix and one rinse, I walked inside again.

"Mom! He's done!"

I heard the stairs creak and Jenny appeared in the doorway, holding her nose. "Do you think it's better?"

"I can't tell," I replied.

She let go of her nose and inhaled tentatively. "It's a lot better, but I think you have to sleep on the couch tonight."

"I'll take a shower and put my underwear in the wash. Maybe that'll be better."

"Throw your underwear in a plastic bag and put them in the outside garbage."

Jeremy was unaccustomed to hearing Jenny address me sternly. He appeared worried. "Are you in trouble, Dad?"

Jenny cut off my reply. "Dad's not in trouble, he's just in need of some…fumigation."

"What's that?"

"It's an old-fashioned process to remove the smell from things."

"Maybe Dad could rub garlic on himself," Jeremy suggested.

"I'm not sure that'd be an improvement, honey."

I trudged upstairs, showered, put on clean clothes, and met Jenny in the dining room. "Is this any better?"

Jenny sniffed the air. "There's still a hint of lutefisk under your aftershave, but it's much better."

"I need to get back to the park for the concert. Are you guys coming along?"

Jenny hesitated a beat too long. "I think we'll drive separately and meet you there. I'm not ready to be trapped in a hot car with you yet."

Chapter Twelve

There were no parking spaces near the park. I walked four blocks with the flute and piccolo cases tucked under my arm. The sidewalks were filled with tourists, and the stores were doing lots of business. People were lined up outside Judy's café and the VFW awaiting seating, and the beer garden was full of people, sitting and standing. A few looked like they might've had more beer than was prudent.

I could hear Doctor Kielbasa playing in the park, and there were people dancing the polka in the street. Overall, it appeared that Buccaneer Days was a booming success. The last polka ended, and the band started packing up their equipment. I met Wendy and the members of the Gin Fizzes behind the bandstand as two men with accordions passed.

Wendy grabbed my arm. "Peter, Where's your pirate costume?"

"I got hit with lutefisk during the lutefisk throwing contest and I was pretty sure none of the band would sit next to me." I pointed to my head. "Only the hat and ostrich plume survived."

Wendy shook her head. "I've been calling your cellphone and leaving messages, but you haven't picked up."

"I think my cellphone may be another casualty of the lutefisk contest. It was slimy when I pulled it out of my pants pocket, and it wouldn't turn on."

"Kevin got food poisoning and we need you to play guitar."

"I've had a long day and I'm committed to playing flute with the city band. I think I need to take a break until then."

Wendy, in her wench outfit, grabbed my arm. "Please."

"I'm sorry, but I'm beat."

"We're getting paid. Your share is fifty bucks."

"I'm just not up for it. Sorry."

She nodded to a back corner of the bandstand and I followed her. "You either play, or I'll make your life a living hell."

I froze, knowing that wouldn't be an idle threat. "You've got nothing on me," I said without conviction. She always had something on me, usually something I was unaware of.

She pulled out her cellphone and flipped through some screens, then held it in front of me. I expected to see something compromising I'd done. Instead I was looking at the naked bodies on the sunbathing cruise. Front and center was Hulda in her bikini, ogling naked men lying face-up on lawn chairs.

I handed the phone back to Wendy, trying to banish the image from my memory. "Did you notice the manscaping?"

I shook my head. "What's manscaping?"

"Those naturists don't go entirely natural. Most of them trim up their...hairy places. The guys said they'd manscaped themselves."

Wendy grabbed the phone, switched the image and stuck it in front of my face. Alma was posed in front of the camera, holding her mink coat open and exposing...everything.

I put up my hand, blocking my view of her phone. "I'd poke my eyes out, but I don't want that to be the last image I see for eternity."

Wendy's smile was wicked. "So, you've seen enough?"

"You can't blackmail me with those pictures. They're not of me and they're on your phone."

Wendy leaned close. "Either you play with my band, or they'll be your computer screen saver until I change it."

Wendy was the computer system administrator for all the Whistling Pines network and could override anything I did. Or she could lock me out of anything she chose to. Hers was no idle threat.

"You wouldn't!"

"Don't test me, Peter."

"Geez, that is underhanded, even for you."

"I do what I have to do."

"I didn't bring a guitar along."

"No problem. Kevin ran for the outhouses and left his guitar and amp here. All you have to do is tune it."

I let out a breath. "I want more out of this than fifty bucks."

Wendy cocked her head. "Like what?"

"Immunity from your blackmail for a year."

"Six months."

"A year, and I want it in writing."

Wendy threw up her hands. "Fine. Write up something next week and I'll sign it."

We set up the equipment and instruments on stage as the crowd gathered. It took a few minutes to tune the unfamiliar electric guitar, but with the organist helping, I got it ready and nodded to Wendy.

Stepping to the microphone, she announced, "We've got a slight change of plans. One of our band members got a bad batch of lutefisk and he's…um…out of sorts." That brought a chuckle. "Peter Rogers, who many of you know, offered to sit in for Kevin."

A round of applause rippled through the crowd, and I felt the familiar warmth of adrenaline, a combination of stage fright, anticipation, and excitement. Wendy nodded to the second microphone, and I stepped forward. She put her hand over her mic and whispered to me, *Ghost Riders in the Sky*.

I played the opening guitar riff and the crowd clapped and hooted. Wendy sang the first verse in her sultry alto voice, and I joined her on the chorus. The world slipped away and I was one with the guitar, the music coming as naturally as breathing. I played the last chord and let the sound echo as the crowd erupted in applause.

Wendy slid next to me and whispered in my ear. "Nice job, sailor."

As much as I hadn't wanted to play, a smile crept over my face and I nodded to her.

We played another half dozen songs I'd done with her band at past gigs, then Wendy walked back to the organist and said something that made him smile. She whispered to the drummer, who had the same response. I was waiting to hear what she had planned, but she walked to the mic.

"Peter and I did this duet earlier this week and it was such a hit I thought we'd repeat it here. I'm splitting the crowd in two and each half of you is going to sing the chorus from *Dead Man's Chest.*

The crowd roared and we had them screaming "Yo ho ho," then, "And a bottle of rum," when Wendy pointed to the alternating halves of the audience. I'd never played for a bigger, rowdier crowd, and it was an incredible rush.

We ended the set with the crowd singing the chorus to *Blow the Man Down* and got a standing ovation. We left the stage, but the applause continued. Jenny and Jeremy met me at the bottom of the steps, Jeremy ready to burst. "Dad, that was epic!"

I hugged him and pecked Jenny's cheek.

Wendy tugged at my arm. "C'mon, we've got to play an encore before the crowd tears down the bandshell."

I was going to protest, but Jenny pushed my shoulder. "Do it." She and Jeremy followed us up the steps and stood hidden in the wings.

The crowd quieted as Wendy stepped to the microphone. "We've never really prepared an encore." She looked at me and shrugged.

I played the opening riff from *I Can't Help Falling in Loving with You*, the song made famous by Elvis. It made a wonderful duet, and I sang the opening. Wendy broke into a wide smile and closed her eyes nodding her head with the beat. She picked up the second stanza, swaying with the music as she sang.

I looked over my shoulder and saw Jenny and Jeremy standing in the wings and realized what I needed to do. I stepped back as I strummed, then hooked Jenny's arm, pulling her to the front of the stage while she shook her head in protest. I'd heard Jenny sing the song in the shower and she knew the words. I hoped she'd be willing to perform in front of the audience...and not kill me for dragging her in front of the crowd.

Wendy and I started the chorus as a duet. I pushed the mic between Jenny and me and nodded for her to sing. She has a lovely soprano voice, but rarely sings outside the shower. She sang a few tentative words. Then, she realized I was singing to her. Only to her. I stared into her eyes and her voice gained strength and confidence and she smiled.

Wendy stepped back, singing softly, her alto voice lending a lovely resonance to Jenny's soprano.

I glanced at the crowd and realized they were silent, rapt. They sensed the electricity and unguarded emotion we were displaying. I glanced at the organist whose eyes were closed, totally into the music. The drummer winked at me, grinning and nodding his head. Everyone in the band knew this was *a moment.* One of those rare, unpredictable times when the band wasn't just singing and playing music, but opening ourselves and pouring out raw emotion.

Wendy stepped forward and waved to the audience, inviting them to join us for the final chorus. Voices quickly joined and the town was filled with the refrain, "I can't help falling in love with you."

I played the last notes, then the applause erupted. Jenny scurried into the wings. The band bowed and we unhooked

274

our electronics. The applause didn't stop so I took Jenny's hand and brought her back onto the stage where the clapping was enhanced by hoots and whistles. She blushed, waved nervously, then pulled away, returning to Jeremy in the wings.

John Carr, the band director, met me on the steps and clapped me on the shoulder. Looking at Jenny and me he said, "That's going to be a tough act to follow."

Jenny's pulled me tight, hugging me over her pregnant tummy. Jeremy looked confused, unsure if his mother was happy or sad. I pulled him into our hug.

Jenny sniffled and dug a tissue out of her pocket. "You shouldn't have done that."

"It was perfect."

Jenny wiped her cheeks. "I'll replay this moment every time I look into your eyes."

Chapter Thirteen

Owens park was a zoo of families, pirates, wenches—many of them intoxicated as Jeremy and Jenny walked out of the bandshell. Ducking into the bandshell's basement, I heard the voices of musicians and a saxophone and oboe tuning for the concert.

The band was mostly there, dressed in variations of pirate costumes, mostly in subdued black, brown, and white. A splash of color in the back corner caught my eye, and when I focused, I realized that Brian was unpacking his antique helicon, a tuba that wraps your torso. The antique horn wasn't surprising, but Brian's parrot costume was beyond eye-catching. He's rather stout, and the colorful costume accentuated his roundness.

I was staring at Brian when a breathy voice said, "I wasn't sure you'd return after the gunfire at the concert you conducted."

I looked away from Brian and into Sheila Peterson's eyes. She was known for wearing overly revealing dresses to the concerts and her pirate's wench costume continued that theme with a short skirt and a bustier that pushed her natural endowment upward into a peasant blouse exposing ivory white cleavage. "Um, hello Sheila. Nice to see you."

She smiled politely. "I heard about your wedding. It sounded…memorable."

"It was." I tried to keep the conversation short and stayed focused on the bridge of her nose so I wouldn't be accused of leering at the cleavage being pressed out of her blouse. "Excuse me, but I need to talk to Brian."

"Um, Peter…"

I turned back to Sheila whose face turned from confident to nervous. "There's someone I want you to meet." She tapped the shoulder of a pirate who was facing away from us. "Mattie…"

The pirate turned, and I recognized Roxanne Matthews who worked at the sporting goods/bait store. Her hair, usually cut short, was wrapped in a bandana and her pirate costume was a basic white shirt, black bolero pants, with knee-high black boots. She'd penciled on a black mustache that looked very out of place on her pretty face.

"Mattie, have you met Peter Rogers?"

Mattie shook my hand. "Sure, he came in the store last December looking for landing nets. Did you catch all the birds?"

"Eventually, but it was a zoo."

Sheila put her arm around Mattie's shoulders and pulled her close to me. She whispered, "Mattie's my partner."

It took a second too long for me to discern the meaning. When I realized they were domestic partners, I reached out, putting a hand on each of their shoulders. "I'm really pleased you've found each other."

Mattie looked around to see if anyone had overheard us. "Um, thanks for saving Sheila at the concert. She said you were a real hero and afterward, you were a gentleman. You gave her the courage to 'come out.' We found each other shortly after that."

I wished them well, then waded through the crowded room to the one splash of bright color among the black and brown costumes. Brian pulled the helicon over his head. "A parrot costume?" I asked.

He smiled. "I've never been one to fade into the wallpaper."

Something squawked in the far corner of the basement and a parrot said, "Polly wants grog."

I looked at Brian. "Who owns the parrot?"

"Frank Abdo has had Pixie for fifteen years. She's really a hoot and likes to bob along with the music. He's going to put her on the stage. She'll bob her head with the beat."

I shook my head. "Okay. Is there anything special I should know?"

"Well, Jessie Bowden had her sex reassignment surgery last month. She's been dressing as a woman for the last year as her body transitioned, but it's final now and the conversion is complete."

I looked around the room, but didn't see Jessie, who had a fine-featured face and had looked entirely comfortable as a woman the last time we'd met. When our eyes met, she walked over and put out her hand. "Peter, it's nice to see you again."

"Hi, Jessie. I heard you're through the process now."

She nodded. "We had a party the night before my surgery to say goodbye to my old self, and now I'm fully transformed into the gender my mind has always known I was meant to be."

I smiled. "I'm very proud of you. It hasn't been an easy transition, and I really hope your life is everything you'd hoped it to be."

Jessie's eyes teared up. "That's about the nicest thing anyone's said to me. Thank you."

I felt a hand on my elbow and Kerry Stone, in his police uniform, steered me to an uncrowded corner as the band started climbing the stairs to the stage. "The park is a zoo. It's jammed shoulder to shoulder, and two thirds of the people are in costume."

"That sounds like a good thing."

Kerry glared at me. "Half the pirates have either a sword and/or pistol jammed in their belts."

"They're replica pistols."

Kerry leaned close. "Most of those replica pistols appear to be capable of firing."

I froze. "And you think the killer might be out there?"

"I don't know if he's in the crowd, and I don't know how dangerous he is."

"There was an incident at the end of the regatta. Dave Carlson threw a line overboard that fouled the Viking boat motor. Then he pushed a bunch of the Viking sailors into the harbor."

Kerry clenched his jaw. "Do you think he's cooled off?"

"I don't know. He might be the person who ran Greg Oien's pickup off the road."

"We haven't seen a black SUV with blackened windows, but I've only got a couple cops here plus the sheriff's department. We're barely able to keep up with the stupid drunks." Kerry paused in thought. "Do you think he'd do something stupid during the concert?"

"His parting words were 'this isn't over.'"

"What does he look like?"

"A pirate."

Kerry clenched his eyes closed and pinched the bridge of his nose. "Any other hint? Maybe his hair color, or the color of his shirt?"

"He pulled a red bandana over his face and his shirt might've been white." I paused. "If it's Dave Carlson, he's got a sword and gun, like a pirate."

"Peter, half the people in town are wearing pirate or wench costumes."

"You can rule out the wenches."

Kerry rolled his eyes. "Gee, thanks. That's really helpful."

"I don't think he'd do anything in a crowd like this."

Signaling John Carr, the three of us edged into a back corner as the band members chattered and tuned their instruments. I leaned close to be heard over the din. "John, it's time to perform *The 1812 Overture.*"

* * *

John got the band's attention, and we took our seats. The park was filled with pirates, wenches, and people in normal dress who'd come to see the pirates and wenches. The band arranged their music as John took the podium and turned on the microphone.

"Ladies, gentlemen, pirates, and wenches. Welcome to the Two Harbors City Band concert. We've chosen an assortment of pirate-themed music and marches for tonight. Our opening number is *The Theme from Pirates of the Caribbean.*"

We moved through several other songs, including a number from *Pirates of Penzance* then, John handed the trumpet player a stack of sheet music and he passed it around as John turned on the microphone.

"We haven't played *The 1812 Overture* for several years, but it came as a special request. I heard clattering on the steps leading to the bandstand and looked through the band, trying to determine the cause of the commotion. As John arranged his music on the podium, two trombone players rolled a small cannon onto the stage. I looked at John who was staring at me with a wide grin. Brian had primed him for the possible additional song.

The flutist sitting next to me saw my confusion and leaned close. "John has a cannon we use for the finale of *The 1812 Overture*."

I looked at the small black cannon and determined the trajectory. "It's aimed at the crowd."

"It's just black powder. It booms and makes a huge cloud of smoke."

John turned to the crowd. "Okay, all ye pirates. I'm dividing you into three groups. You're going to shoot your pistols into the air when I signal for each group at the end."

The crowd was chattering as John turned back toward the band. He signaled for us to raise our instruments. With a downstroke of his baton, we played the opening notes of *The 1812 Overture*. The tempo picked up as the selection progressed.

I searched the crowd for a pirate wearing a red bandana: There were dozens. I looked at each of them, trying to recognize the angry man from the dock. I glanced at the music, making sure I wasn't missing any notes, then looked at another section of audience, checked each person with a red bandana.

The tempo was picking up and I had to concentrate on the music. I glanced up again. A red bandana caught my eye and I realized Dave Carlson, the pirate who'd pushed the Vikings into the harbor, was staring back at me. Dave was a bully, making him unlikely to look away from my stare. If anything, his glare was more menacing than when he'd threatened me on the dock.

I searched for a cop near him. I saw the brown shirt of a county deputy, but he was concentrating on the crowd and wouldn't look up. I finally saw Kerry in the back row. He nodded when our eyes met, and I cast my eyes toward Carlson and his red bandana.

Kerry shrugged, not catching my meaning. I looked at Carlson again, and Kerry glanced over his shoulder trying to see what I was looking at.

Kerry caught my meaning and pushed through a few people. He stepped onto a picnic table and looked at the area I'd indicated.

Carlson felt that something was amiss, and he turned to leave. He elbowed his way through the dozens of people between him and the street behind the park. Noticing Kerry standing on the table, he picked up speed.

The red bandana moving toward the street finally got Kerry's attention. He climbed down from the table and moved through the crowd, taking an angle to cut off Carlson's escape.

As the band approached the finale, John turned toward the crowd and signaled for the pirates to raise their pistols. The band didn't need further direction, playing with fury and intensity as the moment approached when cannons traditionally fired. John waved his baton and pointed at the right portion of the crowd. Rather than the boom of a cannon, there was a staccato banging of pistol fire, a cloud of smoke rising over the crowd. John signaled for the second section to fire. It too offered staccato bangs.

The band was into it, every musician focused and intense, playing loud. Commotion erupted in the rear of the crowd where I expected Kerry to intercept Carlson, but shouting was covered by music and the third wave of pistol fire. The crowd seemed oblivious to whatever was happening behind them.

We played the final bars and John stepped down from the podium. He held a smoldering cedar stick near the cannon and as the last note sounded, he touched the ember to the top of the cannon. The last note echoed in the bandshell. The cannon hissed as the music died, the crowd silent in anticipation of the shot. Sparks flew out of the touch hole, then nothing happened. I looked at John to see what he was going to do, but our conductor seemed content to wait.

After a few seconds, he stepped away and turned on the microphone. "Well, it appears our cannon finale has been a flash in the pan." He glanced at the cannon, which seemed to be done doing whatever it was going to do. John chuckled. "I guess I should've kept my powder dry."

The crowd laughed, and across the street from the park I saw Kerry and another Two Harbors cop wrestling a pirate to the ground. As I'd hoped, Carlson, whose gun was probably loaded with a real lead ball, had retreated when Kerry spotted him. I'd hoped he'd be reluctant to fire his loaded weapon into the air, but in the end, it hadn't mattered. He'd ducked out of the crowd and Kerry was ready to nab him when he ran. From across the crowd Kerry looked back at the band, searching for me. He nodded and gave me a thumbs up when our eyes met.

I heard fluttering on the back of the stage, followed by the parrot spouting a string of expletives worthy of a Marine Corps drill sergeant. The band all turned as a chuckle rose from the crowd. The parrot landed on top of the helicon/tuba bell and was checking out Brian's parrot costume, seemingly evaluating a potential mate.

Frank Abdo, the parrot's owner, stood and tried to coax the bird away from the tuba. He held out a pretzel. "Polly want a cracker?"

Chuck Banks, the other trombone player egged him on. "Give it up, Frank. The bird thinks Brian is a relative."

The parrot eyed the pretzel, then looked at Brian who was waving his arms/wings as if he was trying to take flight. Brian's flapping must've reminded the bird of a mating ritual because Pixie started flapping her wings and hopped onto Brian's shoulder while spewing salty expletives about naked wenches and pirates lusting after them.

With the parrot fixated on Brian as a potential mate, Frank snuck behind them and swept the bird into his arms. That brought out a different string of expletives as they slipped into the wings of the bandshell. Mothers covered their children's ears and the rest of the crowd, many of whom were past tipsy, roared with laughter.

John faced the crowd. "Well, that'll be a topic of discussion at Judy's café for a while." He glanced back at Frank, who was feeding the parrot and talking softly. "As always, we'll close the concert with *Stars and Stripes Forever.* It was written on Christmas Day in 1896 by John Phillip Sousa and adopted as the official march of the United States in

1987." He turned to the band and raised his baton.

With a stroke of John's baton, the band broke into the rousing opening with vigor. From the corner of my eye, I saw something flutter past. The green parrot flew behind the clarinet section and landed on the front edge of the stage. Pixie perched on the stage for a second, her head bobbing to the beat of the music. The crowd roared and clapped. In response, the parrot started strutting down the stage, still bobbing his head to the music. We played on, the parrot pacing the stage, and the crowd clapping along.

I took the piccolo out of my pocket and walked next to the podium. The volume dropped as I started the piccolo solo. The parrot froze, looked at me, then began whistling along with the instrument. The crowd roared, drowning out the music until I trilled at the end of the solo. I stepped away from the podium, the parrot continuing the trill as I walked.

I took my seat as the band's volume rose. I was in the moment, feeling the rush of the music and enjoying the crowd's engagement. The parrot went back to strutting and we played the last bars of Sousa's greatest march. Movement above the crowd caught my eye, and I spotted a squirrel holding a piece of bread between its paws. The last note of the song echoed in the bandshell, and the crowd clapped. The squirrel had my attention. It was gnawing at the filling in a sandwich when John took a bow. The conductor turned and motioned for the band to stand. The clapping slowed and the band members gathered their music. I was intrigued by the squirrel's dexterity as he manipulated the bread between his paws to get at the filling.

Suddenly, there was a hiss and sparks flying out of the cannon's touch hole for a second, then an enormous boom. A cloud of white smoke billowed over the park. The crowd, who'd been folding their chairs and gathering their coolers, roared. The squirrel dropped the bread and scurried up the tree.

I had my instruments and music in hand when there was a shout from the crowd. "I've got it!"

The remaining bandmembers stopped and watched as a woman elbowed her way through the crowd. "I've got the medallion!" She rushed to Meg, who was standing in front of the bandshell. They spoke and Meg led her around the corner.

I was at the top of the steps when Meg rushed up with the woman at her heels. Meg switched on the mic and motioned for the middle-aged woman to join her. "Kathy Laudon found the medallion! Tell them where it was hidden."

Kathy looked confused. "Um, actually, I don't know where it was hidden. It fell in my lap at the end of the concert." She held up a piece of bread, her fingers sticky from peanut butter. "It was in this sandwich that fell out of the tree when the cannon fired."

* * *

Kerry met me at the back of the bandshell. "We arrested Dave Carlson."

"Good job. Your first murder arrest."

Kerry shook his head. "He didn't have a pistol."

"But he ducked out of the crowd before the pirates shot into the air."

"Dave says he ran because you recognized him from the road rage incident. He swears he doesn't own a pistol of any variety."

I frowned. "But he's a competitive hothead. I think he's got a motive to kill the victim."

"It doesn't work unless he had access to a pistol."

"Like I said, I've called all the pawn, antique, and gun shops around the region, and not many black powder pistols have been sold. The recordkeeping is sketchy, because if they're antiques, the buyer doesn't have to go through a federal background check."

"Have there been many sold?"

A handful, and none of them were sold to Dave Carlson." Kerry paused and I saw a glimmer in his eye. "I was focusing on male purchasers. A shop in Silver Bay sold an antique pistol to a woman and I'd blown that off until I searched the national crime database for Colleen West."

"And."

"Colleen West doesn't have a police record, but Colleen McQuarrie, of Bar Harbor Maine has a sealed juvenile record. I've got a call in to the arresting officer."

"Do you think she's smuggling again and killed her husband to cover it up?"

"I can't tie her to a murder weapon and her history is the only thing suggesting she had a role in this."

"Are you going to tell the sheriff or the Ontario police what you've discovered?"

Kerry frowned. "No, I wouldn't want to mess up their ongoing international investigation."

"Do I detect a bit of cynicism creeping into you voice, Chief Stone?"

"I'm trying very hard to maintain my professionalism, but I do know how to swear, and if you keep poking me, I'll singe your ostrich feather with a string of expletives."

I smirked. "Yes sir, Major Stone, sir."

At the edge of his tolerance, Kerry composed himself and smiled with the unscarred half of his face. "Don't push it, sailor."

"I assume this means I can stop looking for a Canadian pirate, eh?"

"You just don't know when to let it go, do you, Peter?"

I looked around, trying to appear innocent. "Excuse me, I think I hear Jenny calling."

Chapter Fourteen

Buccaneer Days was over, and carloads of tourists were leaving town as I drove to work Monday morning. I felt slightly depressed now the festival and concert were over. I sat in my chair and turned on the computer. It was booting up when I sensed someone behind me.

Kerry walked in and sat in my office chair. "Dave Carlson is a hothead."

"What?"

"He owns a construction company and has a sailboat in the harbor."

"And…"

"Dave went on a rant about the victim and how Art and the yacht club were conspiring against him and doing unfair things. Apparently, Art and Colleen West's boat won the regattas whenever Dave raced against them."

"He was eliminating the competition by killing Art?"

Kerry leaned back and shrugged. "He swore he didn't shoot Art."

"Yeah, I can't believe someone would be willing to kill over a sailboat race."

"I spoke with the president of the yacht club. There was more at stake in the races than just bragging rights. Dave negotiated a deal with the manufacturer of his sailboat. If Dave's boat won a regatta or two, the company was going to fly him to the

Caribbean for a race and give his crew matching shirts and jackets with the company logo. Dave told a yacht club member he'd also get a cash bonus for winning."

"You're joking."

Kerry shook his head. "I did a little research into corporate sponsorships and found some are very lucrative. Competitive fishermen get all kinds of perks if they're winning tournaments, as do golfers, tennis players, and more."

"Sailors in Two Harbors? You've got to be kidding!"

"Sporting companies like to have lots of winning teams, regardless of location. They brag about successes in their sales literature and want to claim as many winners as possible."

"But killing someone to get a sail and jacket hardly seems rational."

"Dave didn't kill Art West. But I drafted a letter to the yacht club and the Coast Guard about Dave fouling the Viking ship's propeller and I expect he'll have some problems explaining his justification to them."

"If Dave's not the killer, then you're back to square one."

Kerry closed my office door. "I spoke with the cop who arrested Colleen McQuarrie, now Colleen West, in Maine. As a teenager, she and her boyfriend were buying drugs in Canada and smuggling them back to the U.S. Colleen was convicted of a felony."

"So, she can't own a gun, so she's not the killer either."

Kerry hung his head. "There seems to a loophole in the law. Black powder guns manufactured before 1900 are considered antiques exempt from the court order. They can also be bought and sold by shops without a federal firearms license. Colleen was the woman who bought the pistol from the antiques shop in Silver Bay. They identified her from a picture lineup this morning."

"And…"

"She's in the county jail discussing a plea bargain with her attorney and the county prosecutor."

"Good job, Chief!"

"She and her 'crew' were smuggling drugs. Art didn't know about the smuggling until he found her stash hidden inside a hidden panel when he was tracing the bad wire. His call to her from the boat was to confront her. She went to the marina with the pistol she'd purchased for his pirate costume and shot him, thinking we'd never suspect her."

"Did you find the pistol?"

"It's not at their house or in her car, so I've got divers checking the harbor."

I stood up and shook his hand. Let me treat you to a cup of free coffee to celebrate.

We walked into the dining room in the middle of breakfast. I filled two mugs with coffee and planned to take Kerry back to my office, but saw Howard Johnson waving to us from a table in the back corner.

He pulled out a chair for Kerry. "Chief, it's nice to see you out among your constituents."

Kerry shook Howard's hand and they exchanged names. "Peter invited me down for a cup of coffee."

"I hear you caught a murderer yesterday."

Kerry glanced at me accusingly. I raised my hand in a scout salute. "You just told me."

Howard pushed his breakfast plate aside. "The Whistling Pines rumor mill knew you'd arrested Colleen West before you had her in a jail cell."

Kerry chuckled. "You've got to love a small town." He took a sip of coffee. "What motive does the rumor mill have?"

"She was having an affair with the guy she'd been sailing with." Howard waited for an answer.

Kerry smiled and winked at me. "I can't comment on an ongoing investigation."

Howard nodded. "You can neither confirm, nor deny."

Kerry leaned forward. "You carry yourself like a veteran. I don't recall seeing you at the VFW."

Howard had been reluctant to share details of his military past. He leaned back in his chair. "I limit my visits to the night the VFW serves pasties."

Kerry nodded and extended his left hand, exposing burn scars above his shirt cuff. "Some of us have visible scars, others are easier to hide, but harder to forget."

Howard glanced around, looking at the nearby empty tables, and weighing his words. "Have you heard of the battle of Twin Tunnels?" Kerry and I both shook our heads. "The Chinese Army swarmed over the Korean border. I watched through binoculars and they looked like angry ants erupting out of an anthill that had been poked with a stick. If the weather hadn't broken so the Air Force could fly, we would've been overrun."

Kerry stared at the tabletop. "There are a lot of heroes in times like those."

Howard nodded. "Peter knows. Men do things beyond reason when the chips are down. One of my men won the Medal of Honor," Howard drew a breath, "posthumously."

"You were a platoon commander?" Kerry asked.

"Captain. I had a company."

"You were in the midst of it."

I could see the pain in Howard's eyes as memories flooded back. His response was a nod.

The director rushed into the dining room. Nancy looked around until she spotted me. She threaded her way between tables and put her hand on Kerry's shoulder. "Good morning, chief. I'm glad you're here. You can help Peter get Jenny to the hospital. Her water just broke."

Kerry and I followed Nancy out of the dining room. Jenny was holding hands with an aide as she walked down the hall toward us. I took her hand. "It's time?"

Jenny was amazingly calm, much more so than me. "The contractions are ten minutes apart."

Kerry took Jenny's arm. "I'm parked under the portico."

"It's okay. Peter can drive me."

Kerry was emphatic. "I'm driving."

With Jenny and me in the back seat, Kerry drove carefully through the parking lot. He turned on his flashers when we got to the road. Then he radioed the dispatcher, telling her to have the hospital prepare for a patient about to deliver a baby.

Jenny tensed and lost color as he hung up the mic. She clenched my hand and puffed. The contraction lasted for over a minute. Jenny took a deep breath and looked at me. "I want drugs."

Nurses helped Jenny into a wheelchair as the next contraction hit. Kerry pushed me. "Take care of her. I'll call her parents, then I'll be in."

A nurse handed me disposable scrubs and guided me to a changing room with tiny lockers. Waiting for me when I came out, she led me down the hallway, nearly at a trot. "She's in a birthing room."

A doctor was attending Jenny, who was on a table, her feet in stirrups. I went to her side. "Did you get drugs?"

She shook her head and squeezed my hand as another contraction swept her. She gasped, "It's too late."

The doctor said, "Push!"

Time sped by as the doctor and nurse mumbled. Jenny alternated between squeezing my hand and digging her fingers into my biceps. "This is your fault," she gasped as she pushed again.

She let out a gasp, then relaxed. Almost immediately I heard a baby's cry. A few moments later the nurse rushed to a scale with a blanketed infant wrapped in her arms. The doctor stripped off a pair of blood-stained gloves. "Congratulations, you're the parents of a healthy little girl."

Jenny's tears spilled onto her cheeks and she pulled me close. "You're a daddy."

"I'm a double daddy. Jeremy was hoping for a brother."

"He'll adapt."

The nurse brought the baby to us and laid her in Jenny's arms. She was pink, with fine blonde hair. Jenny rolled the infant so they were face to face. "Hi, little girl. Your daddy and I think your name should be Amelia, after my grandma and your daddy's great grandma." Jenny looked at me. "Do you think she looks like an Amelia?"

I was speechless but croaked, "I think she might like Amy for a nickname."

"Do you want to hold her?"

I must've frozen, but Jenny handled the precious bundle to me.

"Hi, Amy." Her blue eyes searched for me and she squirmed inside the blanket. "You've had a lot of squirming practice. You've been kicking your mommy's bladder for months."

Jenny's parents stood when I entered the waiting room. Jenny's mother rushed to me and took both my hands without speaking. Her eyes searched mine, waiting for news.

"You've got a healthy granddaughter and her name is Amelia. We're going to call her Amy."

I was pulled into an uncharacteristic hug by my mother-in-law. Harold stood smiling, his eyes moist. "Everyone's healthy?" He asked.

"They're great. Jenny's sore and tired. Amy's pink and very active."

* * *

Jenny's parents stayed at Jenny's bedside until Amy became fussy and Jenny decided it was time to feed her. I was sitting next to Jenny's bed as Amy suckled at her mom's breast. I heard bangles knocking together in the hall, presaging my mother's arrival. Mom swept into the room. My mother had announced that she wasn't ready to be a grandmother, but the sight of Amy at Jenny's breast overwhelmed her. She held her hand to her mouth and stood speechless as Jenny covered her breast and wiped the baby's mouth.

"Would you like to hold her, Audrey? Her name is Amelia, named after your grandmother. We're going to call her Amy."

Mother approached the bed and extended her arms. "Yes please."

Watching mother was touching. She cooed and spoke softly. After a few moments she handed Amy back to Jenny, then she nodded me toward the hallway. "I've got a granddaughter."

"You're pleased?"

Mother nodded. "I talked to my financial advisor. I'll set up a college fund for her."

"You have two grandchildren, Mom."

She nodded. "I set one up for Jeremy last January."

"Thank you."

Mother took my hand. "I told you I wasn't ready to be a grandmother. I was wrong. I can't describe how happy this makes me." She paused, then said something I've never heard from her before. "I'm proud of you. I was buried in my projects, but I worried about you. I didn't need to. You've got yourself together."

Approaching footsteps caught my attention. Kerry walked down the hall with Jeremy at his side. They'd become buddies as Jeremy had gotten closer to Kerry's son. Jeremy looked scared and was unusually quiet as he surveyed the unfamiliar hospital surroundings.

He stood next to me, peeking into Jenny's room. "Is Mom in there?"

I pushed him in the door. "Go meet your sister."

Kerry put his arm over my shoulder. "You've done good, sailor."

"I contributed little to this event."

Kerry's focus was inside Jenny's room. Jeremy was sitting on the bed next to Jenny, peeking into the bundle on her chest. "You've built a family."

Mom slid her arm around my waist from the other side. "Yes, dear. You've gone from bachelor to family man in a few short months. I hope you're dealing with the shift in culture."

"I've got this, Mom."

"Peter, come in here," Jenny called.

I walked in with Kerry and mother close behind.

"Kerry, will you take a family photo of us?"

Kerry took out his cellphone and held it up. "I can."

Jenny directed mother and me behind the bed and put Amy in Jeremy's arms, carefully supporting his arms in her forearm.

"Say cheese!"

The flash startled Amy and she cried. Jeremy panicked and handed the baby back to his mom. Kerry held his phone out for photo inspection. "What do you think, Audrey?"

Mom quietly took it, then looked up. "Can you email this photo to me? I'd like to show it to my bridge group this afternoon." She showed the photo to Jenny and me, then we handed the cellphone back to Kerry.

"Give me the email addresses."

Jeremy looked up at me, uninterested in the photo. "Mrs. Stone invited me to sleep over at their house. Is that okay?"

I looked at Kerry, who smiled and nodded.

"Sure."

We walked into the hallway, and I shook Kerry's hand. "Thanks for taking Jeremy tonight."

"You and Jenny need a little time to bond with the baby. We'll make popcorn and watch a movie. Jacob and Jeremy will have a great evening." He didn't rush off, instead looking like he had more to say.

"What's up?"

"It's the Art West investigation."

"It's wrapped up. What about it?"

"I spoke with the harbormaster after our conversation with Jen Flanagan. He set the UPS package on their boat. I asked why he hadn't told me about it the morning we recovered Art's body. He said I hadn't asked specifically about any packages he'd delivered, so he didn't mention it."

"He didn't think you might like to know about it?"

Kerry drew a breath and blew it out. "He suspected it had to do with Jen's activities and he didn't feel the need to mention it. We had a lengthy discussion about illegal activities being my problem, not his, and he pointed out that Jen's cruises were not illegal, just immoral. So, I got in his face and told him it wasn't his place to determine what I should and shouldn't know when I'm investigating a murder. He threw out the phrase, 'what happens on the boat, stays on the boat,' and I replied that did NOT include illegal activities, like drug smuggling or murder."

"And he's onboard with that?"

"More or less. In his defense, Ray told me he blew the whistle on Captain Casey's fish poaching operation. He's not happy about losing Casey's business, but there's a waiting list for boat slips, so he's not really out anything other than the ice he sells to the charter captains for keeping their catches fresh."

Jeremy came out of the room and leaned on the door frame, staring at the baby crib, ending our discussion about police matters.

Kerry removed a small glassine envelope from his breast pocket and held it up. Inside was a tiny brass button. "Edgar gave me a black powder firing cap. If you tell me where you hid the muzzle-loading pistol, I'll take it out north of town and fire it into a swamp." I thought Jeremy was ignoring us, but his sharp hearing caught Kerry's comments. He turned toward us with his eyes gleaming. "Can I shoot it!"

Kerry put the bag back in his pocket. "I've got extra shooting glasses and earplugs. You and Jacob can come along and watch."

"That'll be awesome!"

Kerry walked away, Jeremy at his side, firing questions about shooting the pistol as they left.

My cellphone vibrated in my pocket and I stepped into the hallway, answering the call just before it rolled over to voicemail. "This is Peter."

A nurse walked past, gesturing that phones weren't allowed in the hospital. "Peter, this is Meg."

I walked to a stairwell, hoping the steel door and cement blocks wouldn't block the cell signal. "Meg, what's up?"

"I heard you're a daddy."

"Yes, we had a little girl."

"Everyone is healthy?"

I wasn't interested in having this conversation and responded too sharply. "Yes. Um, Meg, I need to get back…"

"Bear with me for two minutes. I sent your sword to a New York auction house. Their expert inspected it and confirmed the handle is real ivory. It's older than I thought, from the early 1800's. The name etched on the blade was surprising. It was owned by a former Massachusetts governor. If the right people are at the auction, it might sell for several thousand dollars. Do you want to sell it?"

I was stunned. "Yes. Sure."

"I'll let them know. Have fun with your new daughter."

I walked to Jenny's room. Kerry touched my arm as he and Jeremy passed. "Jeremy can stay with us a couple days, until you settle in with the new baby."

"Thanks."

Jenny's parents came back into the room quietly. Howard was beaming and Barbara seemed pleased, but more reserved, probably unwilling to smile because it would cause crow's feet in her carefully applied makeup. Howard shook my hand as Barbara swept past, going to Jenny's side and kissing her on the cheek.

Howard grasped my hand in both of his. "We're overjoyed. A healthy granddaughter and one more Christmas stocking under the mantel."

In the dark of Christmas Eve he'd put a stack of Christmas stockings in front of our fireplace, hinting that he and Barbara would welcome a larger family. They were unaware that Jenny was already pregnant.

"Yes, there'll be another stocking under the fireplace mantel next Christmas."

Howard was slightly less reserved than Barbara, but rarely expressed his opinions. He pulled me close. "And another stocking the following Christmas."

"I think that might be a little too soon."

He pulled me close. "Your biological clocks are ticking."

I smiled. "You and I are not having this discussion."

Howard nodded toward Jenny's bed. Barbara was holding the baby and speaking softly to Jenny. "What do you think they're talking about."

"No. Not Barbara too."

Howard nodded.

The visitors left and I put Amy, who'd fallen asleep, into a crib in the corner. Sitting on the edge of the bed, I swept a stray hair away from Jenny's cheek. "We've got a family."

Jenny nodded. "What did your mother say to you?"

"She's set up college funds for both kids."

Jenny chuckled. "That's what my mom and dad said, too."

I looked at the tiny child in the crib and took a deep breath. "I guess they'll be able to afford any school they want."

Jenny patted my arm. "Are you ready for this?"

"How can I be ready for the unknown?"

"You dealt with Iraq. You'll handle this."

I closed my eyes and the sounds of battle echoed in my head. Jenny's touch brought me back to the room. When I looked into her eyes the visions and smells of Iraq were gone. I nodded, "I think I can handle a dirty diaper."

The End

If you enjoyed this book, please leave a review.

2020 #1 Bestselling Author
Dean Hovey

Dean Hovey is the award-winning and best-selling author of three mystery series. He uses his scientific background, research, travel, and life experience to create life-like characters, gripping storylines, and memorable locations. One reviewer said Dean creates characters he'd like to invite over for a beer and discussion.

Dean and his wife split their year between northern Minnesota and Arizona.

BWL Publishing

bwlpublishing.ca